ALIVE AND KICKING

WORLD WAR II

BOOK THREE

ALIVE AND KICKING

CHRIS LYNCH

★

SCHOLASTIC PRESS ★ NEW YORK

All rights reserved. Published by Scholastic Press,
an imprint of Scholastic Inc., *Publishers since 1920*.
SCHOLASTIC, SCHOLASTIC PRESS, and associated
logos are trademarks and/or registered trademarks of Scholastic Inc.

Library of Congress Cataloging-in-Publication
Data Available

ISBN 978-0-545-52301-1
10 9 8 7 6 5 4 3 2   15 16 17 18 19
Printed in the U.S.A.   23
First edition, February 2015

The text type was set in Sabon.
Book design by Christopher Stengel

CHAPTER ONE

Just Missing

There have been a lot of long roads already since I left home. This one, however, is for sure the longest.

Even though it is the very same road I started out on.

The plane took me to Baltimore. The bus took me to Accokeek, the finest small town in the world. Dropped me at the end of the long cracked road that is now taking me, whether I like it or not, to my house, my parents, and my sister.

I'm here on what they call compassionate leave. As I approach the steps to the front door — the door that opened and closed on every meaningful moment of my life before the Army Air Corps took command of all my moments — I feel like it would be more compassionate to spare me what all I'm about to experience.

Never in my life did I have to walk through that door in fear, whether I was walking inside to face a tough situation, or out. Because I never before had to walk through it without the rock of certainty that was my big brother, Hank, right by my side.

And the first time is the worst time. Hank went down with his ship, the aircraft carrier USS *Yorktown*, when it was sunk in the Pacific at the Battle of Midway.

I'm not here to tell them anything they don't know, since I don't know anything they don't. I am here to be here. To let them see a son. To let them know they still have one, can touch him and squeeze him and feed him and pretend they are keeping him safe and out of harm's way, because we all know that harm's way is way, way over that way. And it is surely not in sweet, sleepy, slow Accokeek, Maryland. Not in this house, where Pop said once that no man should be expected to lose two sons to war. He should be prepared to lose *one* if it came to that, Pop said, and I joked to Hank that that meant him.

It was a joke, because it would never be him. My brother was always that guy, the guy who rose to every challenge. The guy who calmly and quietly worked it all out and then stood up to the invincible school yard bully and showed everybody how invincible the bully wasn't. The guy who flailed as helplessly and repeatedly as the rest of us at the nastiest rising curveball the

Eastern Shore League had ever seen, until he calmly and quietly worked that out, too. I do believe the resulting home run ball still hasn't landed yet, three years after Hank crushed it.

Just like he crushed everything that crossed his path and needed crushing. And everything that crossed my path as well. He was always there for me, a protective two steps ahead of me, and he always saw to it.

Except he's not here now. As I stand in front of this door, the door that always represented the final barrier of safety between us, our family, our home, our peace, and whatever all out there in the world would threaten any of that, I am as fearful as I have ever been at the mere thought of knocking.

He's not here now. Hank. I failed to ever appreciate how profoundly that would hit me. How much he did, even when he didn't seem to be doing anything. I never considered him not being there at my side, so I never got prepared for the first time he wasn't.

And then the first time I have to soldier on without him turns out to be the time I have to talk to the family about soldiering on without him. Indefinitely.

I'm certain they were aware of my approach down

the road. We'd always watched for every movement out those parlor windows since forever. And I'm certain they are aware of my presence here, up the stairs, on the porch, square in front of the door.

And I am certain, once again, of how good and kind these anxious people are, as they wait for me to get my helpless, crying, sad self under control before they make any acknowledgment of my presence.

Good people. They deserve better than what they're getting. They deserve, if nothing else, an explanation. *Why?* for instance. Why their boy? How? How in all of God's creation did we get to this *abomination* of a result? How do righteous, God-fearing folk send not one son but two off into a bloody crusade to preserve decency over evil? To do all the hard-but-right things required to promote a civilization based on God's own love and respect for all our neighbors regardless of their strangeness? How does a stout, unblemished soul like Hank McCallum get knocked off the top deck of one of the world's most resilient, indestructible ships? Especially after he and that ship had already just barely survived another of the deadliest sea battles in history at the Coral Sea only one month before?

Everybody, *everybody* who ever cared about Hank is deserving of an explanation. And all the people who cared about him craziest are inside this house in front of me.

I have some explaining to do.

Even though I have no explanation for them.

As I have no explanation for myself.

And my certainty grows that if Hank were here he would have something to say. Something like an explanation. Hank was always the guy who said those somethings that folks needed to hear.

"The explanation is, there is no explanation," he would have said. And I should say that I don't know this for sure, because no one person knows another enough to speak his thoughts for him. I *should* say that. And I want to say that. I don't know why but something won't let me say it. "Because if you allow it an explanation," he would have said, "that's just a step closer to an excuse. And there is no excuse. Not for all we're doing to each other. No excuse."

I don't know if I ever once seriously disagreed with my big brother, and this right here would be an awkward place to start, but it's probably important to say that I, myself, believe there are sometimes troubles in the world that are so serious and unfair that strong countries are right to come in and do possibly unpleasant violent stuff to defend the weaker countries. Our country just happens to be one of those stronger countries, and I don't think we should have to go around apologizing for that. This war we are fighting is the right war, and we're fighting the right people, without a doubt. This war here — here, there, and everywhere, so it seems — frankly coughs up one scene after another, right in front of your eyes, that makes it blindingly obvious that any sane and moral country has no choice but to intervene.

So then really, ultimately, everything explains itself. It should be easy and straightforward enough to knock on the door and fall into the embrace of my beloved loved ones who've no doubt been storing up hug muscle for two years just for this first contact. And it should be simple, wheezing through love-squashed lungs, to dole out all the plain, heartfelt words, telling them what a hero our hero had been, what magnificent parents they are, how grateful the whole country and the freedom-loving world is for the sacrifice Hank has made and that they have made in giving their oldest son to the Cause, to the United States Navy, and ultimately, to the sea.

It was straightforward, if not easy. And I said it, all of it, to Mam, and to Pop, and to Susan. I practiced it over and over in my head, said it as my duty and for my family, and for peace. We should at least be able to achieve peace here in this one modest house, even if it's the only place on earth we can.

But we can't even manage that, because I cannot say those words about the hero's courage and the family's sacrifice and the country's gratitude and the ocean's satisfaction. I can't say it because it's not so.

Because my brother is not dead. Nobody has shown me otherwise, and in that case I know he has to be alive. Hank McCallum. Ask anybody, they'll back me up on this. Hank McCallum was always gonna be the last man standing at the end of this thing, and if not one person has produced not one item of evidence that my brother was hurt bad at Midway, then you can take it to the bank that he is in one piece somewhere. And even if they did come up with something, well, just don't even bother with it 'cause something's usually nothing in these situations. Show me a whole entire Hank McCallum with maybe a torpedo sticking out of his gut and you will then have my attention, but upon closer inspection, we will all see for ourselves that the toughest, greatest guy who ever lived is still doing exactly that: living. Torpedo or no.

Missing in action is what he is, actually and officially. Lost at sea. He's been lost before, and he'll be lost again.

Because what is missing can be found.

CHAPTER TWO

Threshold

Do you have to make it worse for everyone?" my sister, Susan, says as she yanks the front door open, exposing me frozen in place.

"I didn't do anything, Suzie, what?"

"Twenty minutes, Theo," she says with all the focus I'm lacking. "Twenty minutes you been standing out there, and we're all in here at the windows, and, what, did you forget we had the windows? Did you forget there are people here waiting and anxious while you keep to yourself outside?"

We were so close, me and Susan. Close, like we couldn't pass in the hallway, ever, without one of us poking the other in the side, without maybe me shouldering her into the wall or her jumping on my back.

Now, we stand three feet apart after two years apart, and she is so different already than when I left — tall and strong, and at twelve years old, no more than a couple inches shorter than me. And we stand our distance, stand our ground, until I am propelled forward on the thought that her ground is my ground and my ground is hers, and by the time I wrap my arms fully around her waist she has already pulled me crushingly hard to her, both cracking my neck and talking to it.

"We waited inside as long as we could bear it, Theo. Figured you needed the moment, and then the other moment, and then the moment after . . ."

"All right, girl," I say, just remembering love, right this instant, what it really is, because whatever they say, you do *not* know love anymore when you are separated from this thing right here. Everything else out there is just a blurry picture of it, an IOU of it that just about manages to hold you over till you can come back to the real thing one fine day.

"But when you started crying, Theo . . . I just could not hold myself back, not another second."

"Ah, I wasn't ever crying," I say, playfully pushing her away as we walk together into the living room to face my folks.

"Don't be such a brave jerk," Susan says, holding my hand. "Nobody in this house is gonna think there's a single thing wrong with a man crying when he's been through two years of war like you have."

"Oh, no? Did Mam have a changing of the guard in my absence, or am I still gonna find Pop in his mangy old arm chair with the moss growing over him? 'Cause if he is still there, I think I'll need to keep a stiff lip. He hasn't gone blind, has he?"

The door to the room is closed like they like it, and Susan stops and squeezes both my hands tight enough to make cartilage crackle. She shakes her head at me, silently, over and over again.

"Pop knows how to cry now, Theo. I can tell you that from experience. From a lot of experience. Mam could tell ya as well. So could the lady at the post office, and the congregation of the First Episcopal, and possibly every last crab covering his ears at the bottom of the Chesapeake Bay."

"Oh," I say, staring at this door that is now even scarier than the last one.

The very same doors that were our shields against all fears not long ago.

"Do they even have ears? Theo?"

I turn back toward her, happy for the light air of her voice, for her lively, living, loving-life Suziness regardless of whatever nonsense she's talking. "Who, honey?"

"Crabs," she says. "Ugly, clacky things. Bottom feeders. Don't even look like they should have ears down there, doing all that . . . scuttling they do, oh, Theo . . ." She buries her streaming face in my chest and I hold her head in my hands so hard I could fracture it. I have to find a way through this, and I don't know the way. I'm not even sure what the way is supposed to lead to.

Except for the other side of that door. I know whatever path I am meant to travel for the rest of my life, it goes through that doorway before it can go anywhere else.

"Shall we go in?" I say to my sloppy little sister when she shows no sign of moving from our statue-like, decidedly unstatuesque situation.

That seems to reanimate her, at any rate.

"We?" she says, putting some distance between us with two strong, stiff arms. "I think I'll let *you* be *we* this time. I've been *we* around here for about two years now and I'm a little pooped, to be honest. Especially since . . ." I know she does not mean to leave that important thought unfinished, but it is hardly unfinished all the same. Eventually we are going to have to arrive at the words, but not now. Not yet.

"I know, kid," I say, kissing her forehead and granting her leave. "You've already done enough of this duty without any backup."

"Yes, I have," she says, shuffling to the stairs and up. "And I'm no kid anymore, Theo."

No, she isn't. I wait for her to have cleared the area, I turn, and I knock. A muffled, indistinct sound of welcoming just barely manages to reach me. My mother's voice. I answer to that voice, as ever.

I cannot lie and say there is nothing about entering that old, warm, familiar sitting room that makes me feel better. There is the same low sofa as always, covered in thin fabric as green as a Granny Smith apple. There is nobody on that sofa as Pop occupies one wingback chair to the left of it, and Mam occupies one to the right.

The two of them get up as soon as I enter the room, and despite the full-moon love faces that come beaming my way, I almost wish they'd have stayed in their chairs. At least that way they would have looked right, with their sunken chair-slumped frames fitted correctly to the furniture. But because they are who they are they are bound to get themselves up to greet me proper, and in doing so they look practically as if the chairs came right up off the floor with them, the groaning wooden frames fused right to their own.

"You look wonderful, Mam," I say as I take her in my arms and her gentleman waits politely behind her. She merely moans and holds tighter to me as I shake my pop's hand over her shoulder. "And you too, Pop. Better even than the day I left. I knew you'd be better for being rid of me."

"That is *not* true," Mam snaps harshly, and rightly.

"Sorry, Mam. I'm just so happy to see the two of you with my own eyes, looking so beautiful and strong through everything."

Pop shakes his head sternly at me behind her back where she can't see, and he toggles his hand, two fingers upright and joined as one hard admonishment. "Don't flatter your father, Theo. You know how I feel about flattery, and about honesty."

So much as a cluck of protest would be a mistake right now. He knows flattery and honesty as well as any man alive. He also knows himself, what he does and does not look like.

"Your mother likes it fine, though," he adds. "So keep up the good work while I make the tea."

"All right, Pop. Taking orders is one of my specialties now —"

"And so is speaking charming nonsense to a couple of sad old folks," Mam says warmly, manhandling me down onto the green-apple couch.

"I'll admit to nothing regarding charm, flattery, or nonsense since I entered this house. I say what I see, and that's it."

And I see two beautiful people, who just happen to look like they've seen more war than I have.

I feel oddly, warmly oppressed by the way the two of them stand there looking down on me. They still maintain essentially the whole width of the couch between them, and the *space* of the house is something I am already very conscious of. If I were the middleman right now turning a six-four-three double play, then we would be lined up perfectly.

But we are not turning any double plays here, and it shouldn't be a surprise that nothing is remotely close to perfect. After standing, admiring or assessing me for about the amount of time it would take her to make one of her perfect corned beef sandwiches on marble rye bread, with melted Swiss cheese, sauerkraut, and eye-watering hot English mustard, and big, sour dill pickles on the side, Mam finally breathes some life into this silent, cold room again.

"You must be starving, Theodore," she says, springing into action. "I'll make you a special something," she adds on the fly, trailing the words and the unwellness of it all behind her swinging kitchen door.

Me and Pop, then. The space between these walls, the spaces between these people are now matched by the spaces between words.

What are those words? What can they be? What are they going to have to be?

What *won't* they be? That's the one. Practically the only sure thing I worked out before I got here is that I will not be saying a certain word that I expect everybody else will be saying.

Because he is only MIA. The M is for *missing*. My brother, Seaman Henry "Hank" McCallum of the United States Navy and the Philadelphia Athletics organization, was listed officially as missing in action in the North Pacific on June 6, 1942.

The Japs sunk his ship, but they lost the Battle of Midway. They *lost*. And my thinking is, if they couldn't manage to win, if they couldn't take down any of a number of easier targets with all the advantages they had, there is just no way they had what it would take to finish off a nut as hard as my big brother. So, he's out there, only missing. For now.

"And you wanted to be on that same vessel with him," my father finally says, releasing the words he's had banked up inside there since the moment he opened the letter from the Navy.

"Yes, Pop, I did want to be on the ship with him. And I'd feel the same way about it now. As a matter of fact, I *do* feel the same way about it now. I wish we were together at this minute, like we're supposed to be."

"You wish you were *dead*?" Pop barks, his whole

body so still with contained fury you would swear the sound came from someplace else.

"No, Pop," I say extra calm. "I'd never wish that. What I'm saying is, my brother is missing. And I want to be with him. To help him, the way he always helped me."

I see his face go crimson, his eyes fall. It's not anger now, but it's also not like there's no anger within it.

"There is no way you could help him now, Theodore." He keeps his eyes on the ground for an uncommonly long time. This is a man for whom direct eye contact is both a test and a declaration of a man's character. When he does again look up at me, it is with the acid-stung squint Susan had tried to prepare me for, but that nothing could prepare me for.

Mam comes bumping back through the swinging door, carrying a tray of sandwiches so big she might be expecting me to bring them back for my plane's entire crew. Just like she used to do when a whole mess of us guys were out playing baseball and all I'd done was come in for a glass of water.

She stops short, the door swinging back into the kitchen and then returning to bump her in the backside.

She can't see Pop's eyes from where she is, but she doesn't need to. The room, as well as the house and surely all of Accokeek, is filled with a kind of crying. Like a mist — salty, heavy, and invisible.

Nobody knows what to do. Right down to where to step, where to look, how to even breathe.

"What did you do, Theo?" Susan says, coming in from behind me.

"Nothing," I say. "I didn't *have* to do anything."

"You got them all upset," she says, brushing past me and taking the tray from Mam. "Let's go out to the picnic table. It's nice outside. The air is nice."

"Nice," Mam says, and follows Suzie's lead.

Pop has got concrete feet and shows no ability to move, never mind the will. On her way past, Mam grabs his hand firmly. His head turns in her direction in a strange, unnatural movement that suggests small pulleys and cables at work more than human muscles. But when she nods deeply at him, he moves with her.

The air is nice, like Susan promised, but not as nice as the air here always was before. The sandwiches are somehow better than they ever were, as is the lemonade

Mam must have been squeezing all morning just for this moment.

The moment that is as silent as if we were all cased in cement.

"Still keeping sharp?" Pop finally says. "With the glove, I mean? I suppose there's a lot of boys over there happy to get in a game with a real honest-to-goodness pro ballplayer like yourself, eh? To tell their grandchildren someday, if they make it."

I take a large bite of sandwich, knowingly making real conversation impractical. I shake my head no.

"Why not?" Susan asks sharply.

"Hank has the gloves," I say just after I swallow.

The eyes that widen all around me are not merely surprised eyes. I know what I've said, and the precise way I have said it.

Mam decides to go one way with this. "I'm sure you could find another glove. Another boy, lots of other boys for now. You want to keep your skills sharp, Theo, because there will be a lot of ballplayers coming back soon enough, and anxious to compete for a place —"

Pop goes decidedly the other way. "Those gloves are at the bottom of the ocean, Theo," Dad says sternly. "With our Henry. They went to the bottom of the Pacific with the *Yorktown*. You will need a new glove. You and I, we'll go down to Houston's Hardware and get you a new one before you leave. We'll get you two. Have to keep up your skill level if you want to have any chance of —"

"I'm not thinking about playing ball, Pop. I don't want a new glove, but thank you. I don't even want to pick up a baseball again, not until I see Hank. When I can throw to Hank, and reach him on the fly, that's when I'll play baseball again."

Susan, sitting next to me, across from our parents, leans close and says, "Stop it, Theo." She starts to cry and I can feel it, tears dripping on my ear. "You're just making it worse. Stop it."

"How am I making it worse?" I say. "Seems to me I'm the only one around here trying to make it better."

Pop clears his throat the way a judge pounds a gavel.

"The letter, son . . ." he says, then draws it out of his inside coat pocket.

"Yeah, I know all about this letter, and all the other ones like it, because they're really all the rage these days," I say, because I'm feeling all know-it-all today. The truth is I don't know what to feel or how I could even manage it if I did. I take the letter anyway. And I read.

. . . is to confirm, unfortunately, that your son . . . missing in action since June 6, 1942 . . . the difficulty in not having further information is undoubtedly causing untold additional duress . . . yet you will nevertheless hear from me personally no later than three months from the date of this letter . . .

I begin reading out loud, word for word, until mumbling through some parts starts to seem like a better idea, and then reading anything aloud stops being an option at all.

Susan leans heavily on me as I struggle through to the end. Mam gets up, pats my hands from across the table before wordlessly escaping to her kitchen.

Pop just waits.

He waits an awfully long time, and I am humiliated as I attempt three whole times to tell him what I think about the letter and three times I choke and drown in a sea of little boys' weakness. I am a member of the United States Army Air Forces, for crying out loud. I am made of tougher stuff than this.

"What it says to me," I finally growl to drown out all that other stuff, "is that my brother is missing in action. He is missing, because they haven't found him yet, and he is *in action* because he is Hank McCallum, and that's what he does. He acts. He does, and he *wins*."

I calmly fold the stupid letter back up, hand it ceremoniously to my father. He tucks it into that inside pocket, where it will probably stay indefinitely except for the once or twice a day he takes it out and rereads it for the tiny hint of something better in there that he just missed all the other times.

CHAPTER THREE
Compassionate Leave

I wasn't expecting to be going through this so soon already. But then again, why not?

"Pop," I shout, "you know, you could lighten up a little, since I haven't had anybody smashing tennis balls at me lately."

He nods, then smashes a tennis ball at me harder still. It's the old drill, the one where he would wail away at a barrel of tennis balls, aiming them without pause at Hank and me until we had bruises all over and the agility of a couple of cats.

It's only me now, of course. But Pop being Pop, I never for a second expected him to halve the pace just because there are now only half the hands doing the fielding. He's relentless, running me this way and that along the rear foundation wall of the house. Then as soon as I get something like a rhythm going, he changes up gear, speed, angle, just enough to catch me out, and finally the job is complete when he nails me right in the temple and sends me sprawling. I lay there for several seconds, marveling at his precision and his cunning. I almost turn to my right, where Hank would always be, to say, "Do you believe this guy?" I almost, almost laugh about it together with my brother.

"Not too awful," Pop says as he drags the big barrel over and starts collecting up the balls.

He never did that. No matter how battered and ragged we were, we were always to retrieve every last ball by ourselves.

I'm on my feet, staying close beside him, stooping when he stoops to collect a ball off the ground, rising when he rises to deposit it in the barrel. It becomes impossible not to notice that I'm shadowing him, and he finally looks over my way.

"What gives, Pop?" I ask, squinting hard in case he misses any of my suspicion.

He's about to speak, then waves me off as if this is nothing out of the ordinary. He stoops to pick up another ball and I know this has to be murder on his back because it's hard enough on my own.

"Stop that," Susan says, marching up and taking a

tennis ball right out of our father's hand. "You'll bend over one time too many and you'll be stuck down there."

"Oh, I'm not such an old stiff yet, you know," Pop says as he makes his way toward Mam, who's coming at us with a pitcher of iced tea.

"He tries to do everything himself around here, since you boys shipped out," Susan says. "Up on ladders fixing shutters, cutting away dead branches from the apple trees. Wants to show that he's still the equal of any job that needs doing. But look at him."

"I'm looking," I say. He's kind of bent as he takes the glass of tea from Mam. But then when he should be straightening up again, he just doesn't.

Pop takes a seat on the bench that sits against the wall under the kitchen window.

"Stop staring," Mam says to both Susan and me.

"Sorry, sorry," we both say, realizing we are in fact staring at the proud old guy.

"It's been harder than anything that we have ever been through, son. Harder than anything you could imagine. Some days, I swear to you that if it wasn't for your father and me each being here together, one to egg on the other, I don't think we would get out of that bed at all. It's killing him. Killing us both."

"Ah, Mam," I say and reach out to wrap her up in the firmest hug I've got.

But she remains oddly beyond my grasp. I'm holding her, but I haven't got her all the same.

"What? What is it, Mam?" I say while still trying to hold her the way she is supposed to let me. I can see Susan behind her, looking first strange, then away. She takes the pitcher out of my mother's hand and walks over to Pop.

"No man should be expected to lose two sons to a war," Mam says, echoing Pop's famous phrase.

I stop hugging now, back away a couple of feet.

"What are we talking about here, Mam?"

"You belong here, Theo."

"What?" I yell at my mother for probably the first time in my life. And it brings Pop and Susan hurrying our way. In a state of pure madness that I never would have dreamed before, by the time the four of us are within three feet of one another we are crying our eyes out and arguing fiercely at the same time.

"You just watch your tone when you speak to your mother," Pop wheezes.

"I'm sorry," I say, still too loudly. "But where I *belong* is with my crew, in my aircraft, dropping as many of our bombs and gunning down as many of our enemies as we can manage."

"There is a process for this," Mam says. "We have petitioned the Army, informing them of just how badly we need you . . . now with your brother having —"

"My brother is not dead! Are you listening to me? Is anybody listening to me? He is *missing*, and at some point he won't be, and as far as that *petition* goes, you let somebody whose kid has *died* over there make use of it instead. Because, Mam, Pop, Suzie . . . Hank . . . I love you all but tomorrow morning I am reporting back for duty. And I am going to do whatever it is the Air Corps asks me to do because I know soon enough they are going to station me at a base in England, from where I'm gonna pound the stuffing out of the Nazis and fascists and cowards and sympathizers and anybody else who gets in my way, until none of them are left to kill. And *then* I will know it's time for me, and Hank, to come home, after we've finished the job we were sent to do."

Then it's silent, silent except for my heavy breathing and a lot of snuffling from the three people who have me surrounded as if I'm about to be captured and locked in their prisoner-of-not-going-to-war camp, which is just not going to happen.

I'm right about this, I know I am. And everybody else does, too.

Mam and Pop link arms in an unusual move for them, like they're holding each other upright as they shuffle like a couple of old, old folks back and into the house.

"You know I have to do this, Suzie," I say as she stands there glaring at me.

"I let you get away with it once already," she says. "Now I'm supposed to let it happen again? You have a chance, Theo, to get out of this awful thing. Stay home now. You did your part."

She makes me smile, though that's the last thing she wants. She rushes me, begins pounding on my chest with both fists. And I let her, until after about twenty blows, she finally tires enough to fall into me. I put an arm around her and we walk together back to the house.

The raw truth is I have not done my part yet, or anything even close to it. I have been working the North Atlantic Ferry Service as part of a crew delivering fresh planes overseas just as fast as our factories can build them. In between trips we have been training intensively for the real thing, for when we fly our own Consolidated B-24 Liberator heavy bomber across the sea to a base in the United Kingdom and we don't come right back on some other transport aircraft, because that B-24 will be our plane.

I dream about that several times during the night, there in the comfort of my old bed. But I dream even more about Hank. Hank and me, throwing batting practice to each other, playing long toss through the long days of long summers. I dream about him giving me a good beating over one thing or another, and then once stepping between me and Pop to save me a whole other beating.

You wouldn't take any offer to leave before this war was won, Hank, I know you wouldn't.

And you wouldn't leave me halfway around the world, whether I was missing or fighting or captured or whatever.

I'm doing the right thing because I know it's what you would do. It's how I've always known what to do.

Leaving them is mighty hard, though, brother.

And at least you never had to do it twice.

Compassionate leave. It's a phrase that makes more sense now than ever, as I walk down that same dusty road to catch that same dusty bus to Baltimore. It's barely light out but the three of them are standing in front of the house to wave me off on the trip they never wanted me to take. I wave at them and I love them, and I wave at them some more and then I turn for good, my kit bag weighing me down at the shoulder and my uniform holding me together as a soldier. *So long and be safe and home soon and love and proud* and all the rest of the best words are tugging at my back, and I feel like this longest road ever just grew a little more.

And then I hear her. Her unmistakable flat-footed slap-gallop as my Suzie comes running, trying to catch up to me while Mam tells her just let me go already 'cause the sooner I go the sooner I'm back and Pop says nothing because nothing is all he's got.

And me? I start running. I run, away from Suzie and all that I cannot bear and toward all the unbearable things ahead of me, and as I listen to her positively wail my name, and Hank's, I roar right out loud at all of it, and my mind starts burning with thoughts of the people who are going to pay dearly for all this awfulness.

PART TWO
EUROPE

CHAPTER FOUR

All My Brothers

They are *all* my brothers, is the thing to remember.

I must try to remember.

It shouldn't be difficult, since I find myself muttering exactly that, *they are all my brothers*, as I make my for-real relocation, flying over the Atlantic for the first time without a return ticket. This B-24 Liberator is mine, the one I will be manning for the duration. And this crew, nine of us in all, is the crew I'm going to live or die with. In the month since I ran like a coward away from my little sister, I have spent almost all my waking moments staring at various views of the beautiful United States of America while training to defend it overseas. And those views have been from the most incredible vantage point imaginable, through the glass nose of my B-24. I am the nose gunner of the aircraft, and so the world rushes beneath me at 290 miles per hour. Maryland, New York, New Hampshire, Ohio,

Tennessee, and Georgia each looked as pretty as the last as we came down out of the clouds on all those training runs.

But I have seen enough of home now.

They are all my brothers. I am thinking it as we take off from our base in Oklahoma, and I am still thinking it as we approach our new home, Royal Air Force station Shipdham, in Norfolk, England.

I'm also thinking that Hank shipped out from Norfolk, Virginia. I'm already looking forward to the day we arrange to meet up again and exchange our war stories, and I get to say "So, your Norfolk or mine?" I used to be the funny one in the family. Hope to be again someday.

Got to earn some war stories of my own first, to match up with ol' Hank's.

Anyway, it's a good thing we are all brothers, because working conditions are close. Really, really close. I've never been on a submarine, but I'm almost certain it's roomier than this.

"If you elbow me one more time, boy, I swear . . ." That's the bombardier, Jack Gallagher, yapping at me, the same way he's yapped at me since the day we met.

This ship being a bomber, well the bombardier is fairly important, and they're always quick to let you know that. The bombardier and the navigator both share the same cramped space in the nose cone of a Liberator with the nose gunner, who happens to be the only man out of the three who is not an officer.

They are all my brothers. Even if they are officers.

Fact is, Lieutenant Gallagher doesn't like me, and I don't like him. The navigator, Lieutenant Arthur Bell, is a better guy. I don't like him much, either. Working our way back through the stations of the aircraft, we have the pilot, First Lieutenant Ormston, and the copilot, Lieutenant Lowrie. They ride in a bubble that sits way up on top of the plane above and apart from everybody else. Which pretty much says it all about them and us.

The belly gunner, Sergeant Hargreaves, and the two waist gunners, Sergeant Quinn and Sergeant Dodge, are the exact type of guys you want to have shooting at people who are shooting at you. No more, and no less.

The tail gunner, his name is Boyd. Sergeant Henry Boyd. Some people call him Hank. He is serious, and reliable, tough, has a good enough head on his shoulders that it seems like everybody counts on him and looks up to him, even the officers.

I call him Boyd.

These are my brothers. And we are just now touching down onto the Shipdham tarmac as both the bombardier and the navigator are yelling at me to make more room for them. The space the three of us have to share is like a small greenhouse, toughened glass panels surrounding us and held in place by steel frames that are fitted with .50-caliber machine guns sticking out left, right, and straight ahead as the world hurtles toward us or we hurtle toward it, but it doesn't really matter which because the hurtling has most surely begun either way.

The first thing a person needs to know about England is that the weather is rotten. That's a bad thing if you have to walk around and go to school and pick up groceries for dinner. It's an absolutely diabolical thing if you have to fly an extremely bulky four-engine monster carrying nine crew and up to twelve thousand pounds through constant fog and rain up to your cruising altitude of twenty thousand feet.

And to fly through all that blindly until you emerge into something like daylight, and do it all merely to get into *formation*, requires so much skill, precision, and coordination among men and machines that it's almost unfair to ask us to then go and take that formation into a fight someplace.

But that's just what the job requires.

Our first mission, we're sitting on the runway waiting our turn and the whole of Shipdham feels like an earthquake of giant angry bees coming right up out of the earth beneath us. It's the rumble of five bombardment groups, more than a hundred four-engine heavy bombers all cranked up at once, and it is among the few things that I would say inspires real awe in a guy.

About a quarter of them are B-24D models like mine. The rest are B-17 Flying Fortresses, which are the movie stars of the Eighth Air Force, despite the fact that our ship is bigger, faster, climbs higher, has far greater range, and carries a bigger payload than the Fortress. Actually, it does pretty much *everything* you want and need a long-range heavy bomber to do better than the B-17 does, but to hear guys talk, you'd think that nobody noticed those minor details.

"Have to admit," Lieutenant Bell says as our group pulls into line behind a B-17 group lifting off just ahead of us, "that is one handsome aircraft."

And that is the whole thing right there. The B-24 is not as pretty. A familiar joke from the other crews is that the Liberator is the box that the lovely B-17 Flying Fortress came in. So it gets the *Life Magazine* articles and all that, while we're just here to go about our business of crushing fascism and saving the world and incidental stuff like that.

I hate the B-17. It's like the New York Yankees of the USAAF.

Things are moving along faster now, as the fog has let up just a little bit. We've been inching along at a rate of one takeoff every forty-five seconds — which is a lifetime on a runway when the adrenaline is burning like acid in your chest — but we've pushed it to one every thirty seconds now. The sky is filling up quickly with airpower, although mostly we have to go by the sound since you lose visual contact with each aircraft practically as soon as it leaves the ground.

We are only a few positions from the front now, and if we don't get up there soon, I'm going to explode and set all the other ordnance off as well. The closer we get the more exciting it gets, but the fear is there right along with it. And the cold. That's one flaw of the B-24 we have to acknowledge, is that it's not quite airtight. We don't have a pressurized cabin, which means when we get to ten thousand feet we have to put on our oxygen masks. That, on top of the gear, which in my case is the full head-to-toe leathers, with the lamb's-wool lining. We have the choice of that or the electrically heated flight suits that some of the guys are wearing, but after one too many stories of them shorting out and even catching fire, I decided I would live and die with the hides of good old American farm beasts wrapped around me.

"Here we go, boys," First Lieutenant Ormston announces over the radio as we watch our group's assembly ship take off, then our lead ship, then hear our own four beautiful brute engines begin that crazy revving up and up that rattles your ribs and tells your heart you are about to sky.

It's almost unbearable, the roaring, rattling, juddering sensation as we get up to speed and then off the ground, following nothing we can see. Quickly, we bank left as the big bird simultaneously climbs and goes into the wide racetrack oval pattern that every other plane is flying in just as blindly. There will be no more radio communication until we all finally get into formation, so it feels like pretty hairy business before we even get to the fighting part.

"What's the point of the radio silence anyway?" I say as I lean hard into the farthest forward reaches of my glass nose cone to see whatever I might see.

"Well, because we'd all kinda like to reach the target zone before getting the whole bunch of us blasted back to the ground, knucklehead."

That's Lieutenant Gallagher, whom I was *not* asking.

"Think about it, McCallum," Lieutenant Bell says. Being a navigator he tends to answer questions with more fact and less jerk than certain other crew members. "I mean, occupied Europe — which means, basically, one big, giant Nazi Germany — is *right there*." He points from his position on my left, across to the equally gray and indistinct swirl of sky on my right. You can't even see *right there* right there, so his point is a little washed out.

"They monitor everything all along the English Coast," Gallagher snaps. "Probably hearing this conversation right now, so maybe you should button your lip before they realize what a green bunch of dummies we've got for gunners on these boats."

The military has a lot of rules, to keep order. That is understandable. That is also the only reason Lieutenant Gallagher isn't collecting his teeth up off the floor of our cozy compartment right now. I'm going to have to find a way around some rules before all this is over.

The target zone itself almost doesn't count as a long-distance bombing run. We are headed for a heavy industrial part of France, near the Belgian border — in other words, as Bell might say, the nearest edge of Hitler's Europe. Our targets are steelworks, engineering factories, and railroad manufacturing operations. It almost feels like we are bullying fat duck targets that are just gonna squat there while this force of nature swoops down to pound them into dust. But, they started it.

It is bone-cracking cold already as Bell informs the pilot that we are within fifteen minutes of clearing cloud cover. It has taken over an hour of ovalling just to get us this far, and the low groans of approval heard throughout the ship show just how little it will take now to get us enthusiastic again. I have never been so cold. Gallagher and Bell, on either side of me, are wearing the heated suits, though the small amount of heat I can sense off them must be more than they themselves are feeling. They are shivering and punching themselves to keep warm.

We have all got our gas masks on now, and the air is very thin as the Liberator bursts through the last of the cloud cover into brilliant sunny sky. My heart jumps. It feels like I am the very tip of a rocket, flying at the front point of the plane, nothing but glass between me and the incredible sight of a hundred heavy bombers swarming and finding formation twenty thousand feet above earth.

First we locate the assembly ship for our bombardment group. There are five BGs on this mission and each flies its own assembly ship that is decorated in some wild pattern or other strictly for the purpose of getting each group gathered as quickly as possible, and then for the groups to assume the overall formation as we embark on our assignment. Achieving, and maintaining, the strict formations that are key to the success of any raid with these great numbers of massive planes is complicated enough to hurt my head and make me glad to be nothing more than a machine gunner.

We find our assembly ship instantly, with its checkerboard paint scheme, and within minutes my twelve-plane squadron is assembled and then linked up with the three others that make up our BG. In no time, the other four groups have done the same and we see all four crazy-quilt assembly ships bank away with their zebra stripes and polka dots and head back to base. That leaves each group's lead ship now in charge as the full in-formation assault team tears across the sky and across the English Channel to finally see what damage we can do.

There has never been anything like this in my experience. We have done hours and hours of training at high altitude, target shooting, mock bombing runs, and learning the fine art of formation flying. But that had been with our own squadron, then with several, which made the deal complicated enough. But this, this field of airpower we're marshaling now, is at least three times the size of any grouping I've ever even seen. Here above the clouds we absolutely own the entire sky. I get a rush of a feeling that we cannot get to the target area fast enough because we are, frankly, unbeatable the way we are right now. I keep sneaking peeks, like a tourist or something, looking at the big bombers either side of us, way off ahead, beneath us and above us. The greenhouse canopy under which I work has to be the most remarkable theater seat in the whole world. Or above it.

"Eyes on the road, batboy," Gallagher snaps, looking up at me from his station right down on the floor. He's already at the bomb sight. He's at the center, really, of everything we do on this ship. I'd hate to ever say it to his face, but he is pretty much indispensable, doing all the fine-tune calculations to make sure when we go out to bomb something it gets bombed. Otherwise we have been a big, fat flying nothing just wasting resources in the sky. There is even a point where the bombardier actually has control of the aircraft itself for the crucial seconds prior to dropping our load, after which he graciously gives the pilot something to do again.

Still, from where he is, at my feet, I could give him a pretty good kicking without the mission necessarily losing anything.

"Really, McCallum, eyes straight ahead now, total focus," Bell says from behind me, where he's taken up his position at the navigator's table.

You can feel it, even if we still can't see anything except us. Us, and us and more us in every direction. Pilot Ormston chirps his directions and updates in as chopped a manner as possible, never wasting an extra second on chitchat, and he communicates a lot with it all the same. "Descending," he says sharply, and we all sure feel it now.

I am gripping the handles too tightly on my .50-caliber machine gun and staring as straight as my bulging eyes can manage. The compartment has three of these weapons fitted into the nose structure, and the truth is, you'd need all three to be able to cover all the necessary angles to defend this section of the aircraft competently. My only strategy is to approach it like I did in the Eastern Shore League when I had to face a pitcher with a ninety-five-mile-per-hour fastball and only limited control of it: dig in, don't flinch, just flat out guess on the location, and above all, start swinging at the first twitch of motion.

Hank hated that method when I told him about it. He probably hated more that most of the time my guesses were spookily accurate.

"Whose idea was this daylight raiding thing again?" Gallagher growls, peering steadily through his bombsight.

"Wasn't mine, I can tell you that," I say.

"Well, that rules out the batboy as the number one suspect," he sneers, using a hated nickname that is establishing itself far too securely. I never even told anybody about my playing in the A's system, so the rat must have his own intelligence sources. I'd like to thank all involved with a couple of knuckle sandwiches.

As the whole formation starts diving at an even steeper angle, still above the cloud layer, another big collective sound joins in with the thunderous roar of our engines.

"What am I hearing?" I call out, my rookie nerves overriding training and composure.

"Fighters!" Lieutenant Ormston snaps.

"From every corner!" Couley, the engineer, adds.

"I guess we can assume they're not ours," Bell jokes, slapping his navigator's table with a vicious laugh.

That's one thing American bombardment crews are always questioning, and British crews are always mocking, about USAAF strategy in this theater of the war. We're the only ones crazy enough to go out bombing in whatever passes for daylight here. And, for the most part, we do it without any fighter escorts looking out for us along the way.

We can do anything, under any conditions, without needing any ol' *escorts*, either. I guess.

"Dead ahead, three o'clock, twelve o'clock, seven o'clock!" Lowrie the copilot yowls.

All in one devilish, magical moment, the sky opens wide up below and before us like there was never any cloud littering this sky today. And the air all around fills with enemy fighter planes, Messerschmitt Bf 109s, Focke-Wulf 190s. There is a trio of them scorching so directly toward the very tip of the nose of this plane you could swear they had it out for me personally.

Batatatatatatatata. Battattaataatatatatatataa!

My entire body feels it as the Browning .50s pound the air and the Luftwaffe fighters with more fury than I could ever ask for. Two of the three fighters peel off left and right, as the third keeps bearing down like he's intending to come right through the window. He's firing away exactly as I am and I hear several large rounds ping and zing off the fuselage before I score big, getting a bead on the underside of his left wing and riddling it as he banks straight up over my head. The engineer's position behind our pilot has its own gun turret and he picks the guy up as I concentrate on the next flurry coming on.

The whole ship is ringing with machine-gun fire from both waist gunners, myself, topside from Couley, and holding the fort way at the back, tail gunner Boyd.

Suddenly it's a bit more crowded but I don't mind too much since it's Bell, away from his table and manning the left-side machine gun, blasting away at the same bunch targeting me. There is a third gun mounted to my right, but Gallagher is completely glued to his primary concern. That bomb sight on the floor is his only view of the world at this moment.

The German fighters are fast and dodgy, but the Liberator is packed with a lot of firepower for a strategic bomber, so we give as good as we get. But their ability to penetrate into, and move almost effortlessly within, our immense and precise formation, is more than a little bit unnerving. They appear and disappear like speedy nightmares, drilling rounds into our wing and side sections before vanishing and reappearing on the other side of the plane, or just above it. And there seem to be hundreds of them.

I jump from the center gun to the right-side one when threats increase over there. Through all the smoky chaos, Gallagher remains deadly zoned in and applied to his task, our task.

And despite the fierce resistance designed to at least disrupt our progress, with every passing second we are closer to our targets. We can see them now. We can *see* the factories and the steelworks that soon nobody will ever see again.

"I love daylight raids!" I yell, just about over the sound of my guns as I pepper the side of a Messerschmitt so close I could have spat on the pilot's face if I could have gotten my window open. I see him trailing something, heavy fluid in a steady stream, as he spins away and limps out of the fight for today, or maybe forever if it all works out right. The thrill I feel at the sight of the failing plane, at *my* lethal work, makes me want to break away somehow and follow him till I can witness the fantastic, awful end. I hope the plane dies. I hope the Nazi fighter pilot dies. And I hope he manages to take out three or four more of them when he hits the ground.

"I'm killin' 'em, Suzie," I say as I switch back again to the center gun, "just like you said to."

I wonder if Hank's gotten to kill anybody. Most likely not. His station, his situation, chances wouldn't come along all that often. It makes me sad for him, and more murderous, too.

"Hang on boys, hang on, doin' great! Keep it up!" That's Gallagher, his eye sockets essentially welded onto the sight's eyepiece. He smells blood, and we just have to get him to it.

But that is proving to be a lot harder than I'd have thought. These fighters, kids' toys next to the bulk of what we brought, are disrupting everything we do. The precision of the formation, so critical to the bombing strategy, is getting pushed and unbalanced by the relentlessness of the fighters' attacks. There is firepower of all kinds filling the air, bringing yet another shade of gray to these smoky skies, and we are in a real dogfight to the death.

There is a shocking great crack and commotion as two Liberators ahead get drawn just far enough out of their assigned patterns to clip wings. One of the planes dips sharply in the direction of the ground while the other struggles back into position.

The diving plane is trailing smoke from one sputtering engine as the pilot wrangles it level but flies his ship back in the direction we came from. He's flying straight into the face of our formation for a breathless moment before diving lower still and sailing beneath us.

The formation is off, some squadrons drifting farther out to the perimeter than they should, as we press on to the targets below while fighting off the devils above.

"Lining her up, Lieutenant!" Gallagher calls at the very instant we hear the first note of that unique and beautiful song of bombs whistling down. Our lead ship has opened up bomb bay doors and is letting fly with a blizzard of five-hundred-pound bombs that are racing down, then *p-pow p-pow-p-pow pow pow* exploding, decimating the railroad operation that for only a few seconds looks just like the recon diagrams we studied. In an instant, it looks like fire, rubble, and not much else.

Our group banks beautifully, like we are one perfect steel creature on the wind, off to the coordinates to the east, just there, where the time comes. Gallagher takes over, hollering like a madman as the bomb bay doors open wide, the whistlers sing all the way to their destination. And again, *p-pow p-powpowpow*, the eruptions as those vital war-machine facilities pop right off the map.

As we sail over the top of them, one after another of our assigned targets takes the pounding. The dogged Messerschmitt and Wulf fighters clearly don't want to concede and they fight us even as we make our sweeping arc to leave. Boyd gets most of the action now as the fighters get a good long look at our elite fleet, tail-gunner style, and you can finally feel the fuel running out of this scrappy firefight.

But a fight it was. My first live combat.

I collapse involuntarily as my knees finally reveal all that my nervous system has been through.

"Ha!" Gallagher says when he finds me wedged down there in his world.

"So, this is how it's gonna be, huh?" I say to him.

"Oh, yeah," he says, laughing a degree or two less meanly than usual. "This, and then this again, then a whole lot more this waiting behind it."

"It is a very flawed aircraft," Bell says grimly.

"So, what do you care if it's fat and ugly?" Gallagher says.

"I don't," he says. "But I do care that it's a lot harder to maneuver in tight formation than the Fortress is. I care about that a lot."

Gallagher laughs some more as I climb up off the floor, and I start to think that this post-bombing Gallagher is kind of giddy and freakish, with weird energy to burn away. I prefer this version. I hope we drop nonstop ordnance everywhere, just to make the working atmosphere around here a bit more fun.

"I can handle this aircraft, Lieutenant Bell," Ormston surprises us all by kind of yelling. "Whatever she requires, your pilot and copilot are equal to the task, and if you don't feel you can have confidence in that, then you are free to seek a transfer whenever you like."

"It was not a criticism of personnel, sir," Bell says without turning back in Ormston's direction.

"Well, if you don't mind, I think morale might be better served if you don't critique the ship. Certainly not while she's not even had a chance to catch her breath after such a battle."

Gallagher is still at it. "Well, to be fair, sir, she could maybe breathe a little better if she wasn't so fat and ugly."

There is no acknowledgment at all from the pilots' station.

"I happen to think she's beautiful," I say to Gallagher. Bell is hunched over his navigator's table again.

"Well, that's good, McCallum. It really is a fine thing. Especially since you're the guy most likely to be stuck with her. *Go down with the ship*, as the saying goes."

"Oh," I say, trying to act even colder than I am, which would be a temperature that probably doesn't even exist. "The Flying Coffin thing? Big deal."

"That is enough, gentlemen," Ormston declares. "McCallum, armaments check, work your way from the tail on up. If we have to fight again in twenty minutes, you see that we're loaded up and ready."

Since it feels like I've been trapped in that tiny asylum greenhouse with the front-of-house guys for a whole month, a little round-the-ship inventory sounds just fine to me.

For some strange reason that probably makes sense to him, Gallagher decides to follow behind like my assistant or something as I work my way along the narrow spaces toward the tiny catwalk that connects the front of the plane with the rear, over the bomb bay.

"What are you doing, Lieutenant Gallagher?" Ormston wants to know since he is the boss and all.

"Thought I'd go for a little stretch, too. Gets kinda squirrelly up there in the compartment, as you can imagine."

"Lieutenant," Ormston huffs, "I don't believe you could imagine the things I can imagine. And I'm sure I don't want to imagine what you can imagine. So we'll just leave out the suspense. Go back and man that nose gun."

That does make me want to let out a little victory laugh, but Gallagher himself beats me to it. Louder and nutsier than I would have laughed to boot.

"Stuck in the nose of the Flying Coffin," he says, mock serious. "You might have a point there, Bell, about the curious construction of this beast. Surely there should be more than one way out."

There is only one exit from which to bail out, because it's the only exit big enough for a man wearing a parachute to fit through. That escape is at the tail gunner's position, as far away as it could be from the nose gunner's.

CHAPTER FIVE

We Ain't No Moles

Every bomber has its own nickname and artwork painted along one or both sides of the nose. It's unofficial stuff, purely down to the crews themselves, but once it's on there it stays there until the guys crash the artwork into the side of a mountain or the bottom of an ocean. I don't know when it happened or how it was decided, but as I approach the plane one crisp, clear November morning, there it is.

BATBOY. And the painted image is of a kid in a too-large baseball uniform, smiling out at the world as he swings at an also too-large baseball, missing it by a country mile. The quality of the art is at about cave-painting level but there is no missing the expression on the batter, who looks like he's taken one too many fastballs to the coconut.

I stand for ages looking at the thing, not entirely sure I am even really seeing this image on this plane.

The next man out is our engineer, Sergeant Couley.

"What do you know about this, Couley?" I ask.

"Me? I'm the one guy who knows everything about this plane."

Since Couley seems satisfied with the incompleteness of that answer, I think maybe some nudging is in order.

"Who put it there, Couley, is what I mean? Who decided? Was there a meeting I missed or something where this was voted on?"

He sighs, puts a fatherly hand on my shoulder, even though he's barely older than me, and says, "I said I knew everything about the plane, McCallum. Now you're asking me about art and politics and everything that just makes things messier. Listen, do yourself a favor. Point, and shoot. Keep it simple. Point and shoot and leave everything else to everybody else and you'll do just fine."

He walks then toward the plane's tail to climb inside and start his routine of checking over each little detail and then each detail within that detail two or three times over before most guys have even finished chow. I follow him inside.

When I catch up to him swiveling Boyd's tail gunner turret back and forth rapidly to test its responsiveness, he looks right up and gives me a grin.

"What I do know is that every man on this crew is a real baseball fan. So, maybe if I were you I'd take it as a kind of compliment. We love the game and we're pleased to have a certified somebody who's played ball at a high level on our team."

That stops me short enough. As a guy who swore not to say another word about baseball out loud until the day he could say it to his brother, I should probably be ashamed of how proud and — as Mam would surely point out — *immodest* I became just a few seconds ago. US Army Air Force Engineer, Gunner, Sergeant George Couley has turned a pretty neat trick there.

It takes him only those few words, those few seconds, to defuse a small flint of something I've been letting burn at the center of my guts. A flint of lots of somethings, probably, that have just been feeding on themselves until probably they would've burnt me up completely from the inside on out. A few words and a few seconds was enough for just one guy to replace that burning with a little ball of pride.

And then, it takes him even fewer words and seconds to poke it into something else altogether. "Even though, y'know, really, the A's? The A's *lower-level* farm team to boot?"

His tone is meant, I think, to convey pity for what I went through back in the trenches of Federalsburg. I'm not biting.

"Yeah," I say. "Eastern Shore League. Not so glamorous, maybe, but plenty scrappy. Produced quite a few fine ballplayers who went on to bigger things. Mickey Vernon came out of the Eastern Shore. Carl Furillo. Jimmie Foxx. You know Jimmie Foxx? Don't get much bigger than Double X, I'll tell ya that."

"Whoa, whoa," Couley says, putting both hands on my shoulders to calm me down, though it makes me even edgier to feel his grip. "I believe you that it's a beautiful part of the world, hardworking league, all that. I simply hope they work some actual farms on those lower-level farm teams, so they could be tending spinach or carrots or something good for society on those fields, in between dropping routine fly balls and swinging at 3-and-0 curveballs in the dirt."

There was a time when I would have had a snappy comeback for this. And I would have even had fun delivering it. But, I feel like a pitcher standing on the mound who knows he hasn't got his good stuff going for him and has no idea if it's coming back.

I try to pull my shoulders from his hands, stepping sideways, but he surprises me by stepping right with me, like it's a dance or something. And still, there are those hands gripping these shoulders.

"It's just a little needlin', McCallum, that's all. It's practically required around here, trapped with this bunch of salamis, trying to kill half the world before they kill our half. It'll make ya bananas if ya don't sometimes think of dumb stuff to say just to fill the air-spaces. Right? I mean, right?"

I am, I'm afraid, getting a little of the bananas business he refers to. But I also didn't think I was making it anybody else's problem.

"Right," I say, happier than a professional world-class gunman should probably sound. "Right, I was just giving it back to ya. I was playing a higher level of ball than, what, ninety-five percent of players ever reach.

And if this wicked, stupid . . . thing didn't come along and stop everybody's world right in their tracks . . ."

"Exactly. And you are still a young pup. You'll start climbing your way back to the top again. You'll be aces and life will be perfect for elite talent like yourself. Once we get this job here done right first, however."

I nod, with some force, and likewise remove Couley's hands from my shoulders.

"Thanks," I say.

"You're welcome. But you already must know any one of us would club you in the street with your own bat to get where you got. Even, with, well, you know."

"That's a sorry mark of things," I say. "Here I am all the way over in England, spending much of my time at twenty or twenty-five thousand feet, shooting all the bad guys. Then I'm discovered to be a professional prospect in America's greatest sport . . . the sport that we are all here fighting for, by the way . . . and some-how the whole deal tumbles because I'm followed by the Philadelphia Athletics' *worldwide* reputation for stinking so bad, so often."

Couley makes a sound that's as much like a shrug as anything and turns his attention again to the tail turret, which makes a faint grinding noise when the guns are turned straight up.

"I have to tell you something," says Boyd, the tail gunner himself, as he pops through the rear opening right next to his place of work. He seems fairly grim and serious in his manner and expression, and reflexively I find myself mirroring all that.

"Okay," I say.

"Well, I think you should take that hard luck story of yours, with the horror of being a prisoner of the historically hopeless baseball club that is the Philadelphia DOA's and try telling it around, just for fun, to see how much sympathy you get. I'd love to hear the opinions you'd get out of the Europeans we've come to save from all the misery they've been suffering though. Unfortunately we've had to also obliterate a good bit of history and culture and people and stuff in the process."

And at this point, this is where I know I should take a snap-crack at Sergeant Boyd. The same Boyd who is usually counted among the decents and bearables, but seems to have had a nasty fall off his very high horse this morning as he made his way to the noble and reliable Batboy.

But, I don't have the goods for him. Wherever those goods currently are they are locked away securely and I don't have access. I still have the power of staring, staring stupidly and at length, however. So I give him that. There.

I would say that Sergeant Boyd is unmoved by my steely and stealthy act of aggression beamed across the few feet of space separating us. But that is not the case. The stare he offers in return is total incomprehension. *Studied* incomprehension, which is even better because he's trying to work me out and is failing.

Sergeant Couley may or may not have solved the noise issue that bothered him, but either way, he rises from his engineer's fidgety fix-it-all crouch and pivots smoothly around and into the tail gunner's battle station, hands on guns, feet on floor pedals, shifting slightly my way, or Boyd's way, or both.

"It's very . . . adversarial in here today, men. Can you feel it? I can feel it, and I started it, so I should know. Nobody feels too great about anything right now, as everybody is aware. Our first mission as a group was, in the complicated dialect of the military, a 'less than optimal, however successful, outcome.' We here in the armed services of course understand the English translation to be that basically we took a whole lot of industrial muscle to perform a pretty straightforward hammer job, all in an effort to terrify our enemies into understanding that we — the long-anticipated units of the US Army Air Forces — mean business in the same way as God means business with His heavy artillery. God has famine, and pestilence, and floods and so on. While we, bring War. We bring it with more resources, more innovation, and more raw firepower than any force in history. Short, naturally, of God. But the other big difference is, when God goes after you with, maybe locusts or something, well, you just consider yourself beaten from the get-go, wiped out, barren, and left with running away as the only option open to you, provided God is even in that soft a mood, which isn't often in the year of our Lord 1942 and you happen to be Jewish or Chinese or Polish or taller than Adolph Hitler or moored minding your own business at Pearl Harbor, to mention just a few of the unchosen people of our times."

Then there is a pause, which is as welcome to me as it probably is to Boyd. Though I'm not sure for Couley it is even intentional. He's distractedly messing with a mounted pair of Browning .50 caliber machine guns, like you do when you are trying so hard to regain your train of thought that you could just . . . scream, we hope, or possibly flex your fingers a little too much.

"You were pointing out everybody's tense right now," I say.

"And," Boyd adds, "pointing out the way to tell the difference between you and God."

"Right, that's the critical thing, though no, smart guy, I didn't say between myself and God. The difference is between the world's most powerful and righteous militarized force for good — and please don't need me to tell you who that is — and the Almighty Himself when He, too, gets a notion that someone doing evil needs smiting." Couley takes a breath, pausing long enough to register we are all but scratching our heads at this. "Oh, stop pretending with those looks," he says, " 'cause you both know exactly what I'm saying. When God goes to the effort of bringing almighty wrath to your door, your door is no more. God doesn't leave you just a little upset, and with some bruising to your cheek when you provoke His fury. God does not walk away from administering His terrible swift vengeance with a blackened eye and a bloody nose out of the bargain, does He?"

At this instant I'm not too disappointed that my wisecracking impulse has gone AWOL because I have no interest in seeing how far Couley is liable to take this. And if my impulse was back with me I would without a doubt aim it at twelve o'clock high and probably end up with that bloody nose myself. With the mouth I used to have on me, I was usually asking for that type of response. Of course, back then I always had backup.

"I wouldn't think He would, no," Boyd says agreeably.

"Nope, He would surely not," Couley says. "But we absolutely did. Half our fleet got shot up enough to delay at least two operations over the past week while they got patched."

"Yeah," I say, turning away. I don't like this turn, the truth of it, the fact and the feeling, the *failure* of execution that allowed that batch of nasty little German fighter birds to create such a smoke-and-bullet ballet that we did no more than a quarter of the damage we'd been sent to France to carry out. The damage we left in our wake tallied way, way less than we thought we saw through the smoke, and the bullets, and the bold, fear-less, distracting manner with which they took the fight to us and took true victory away.

Not only that, which would have been humiliation enough. They also took the opportunity we gave them and put a gleaming, magnificent machine, one of our Flying Fortresses from the 392nd BG, right down into the English Channel, with her whole crew of ten dedi-cated men taking the trip with her to the bottom.

Planes go down. They tell us that every day of our Air Corps lives. I know that as well as the guys — and there are lots of them around here — who have seen it happen right in front of their eyes, watched fifty planes and five hundred crewmen crushed and thrown and incinerated and butchered in fifty different horrifying ways. But for the past week I have not seen a single face on any corner of the base at Shipdham that didn't burn with the same burn that I have been feeling and wear-ing since that Flying Fortress fell.

"McCallum, don't leave," Boyd calls after I have obviously already left. I have weaved my way up the tight passageway that regularly takes me from the tail gunner's solitary nest up to the waist of the Liberator, where both side guns and the belly and top turret weapons are clustered in a sort of rapid-fire neighborhood, then on to the comparative luxury of the flight deck, where the pilot and copilot's seats are heated and armored and rumored to be as expertly padded as they look. I have never sat in one myself. The engineer's top turret perch is secured right up close behind the flight deck thrones of the plane's exalted command class, but proximity is about the only thing they share in this rigid little society of ours.

I take a few deep breaths and return to the tail end, to the two men who happen to make a living shooting Messerschmitt 109s and Focke-Wulf 190s, just like I do. We shoot at threatening things so our people can drop our bombs correctly and accurately on other dangerous things, while we all coexist inside this Batboy we seem to have inherited, or made, invented, or maybe were swallowed whole by.

"We talked about it and we agreed," Sergeant Couley says, "that any team you played on must have had something going for it. You would have been a formidable opponent, and tough to play against. By which I mean, jokes are just jokes, but this here, is respect."

I am glad, now, that I made the trip back. But I stay on the edge of the small catwalk that I just walked and will walk again, back to the farthest point, where I belong. The two of them are slumped over Boyd's guns in a kind of loungey way that I don't quite understand because they exist where they do and so do I. Every man in his place is an article of faith here, crucial to the smooth running of a thing like this thing. Batboy.

I wave that uncommitted short-arm wave that must come over more like a request to go rather than a signal that that is what you are doing regardless.

Couley raises one stiff arm, as if he's taking some solemn oath, so I figure that's to be taken as a wave. Boyd tacks a different way entirely, which seems like a thing I should expect from him. Boyd chooses, rather than a stiff or even a motional wave, to point at me, very hard, definitively, not quite accusingly, but directly would be a fair description.

"It's not your fault," Boyd says, his stare bearing on me.

I'm not even close to thinking I know what he's referring to. So it doesn't make sense when something in it not only makes me choke up just like that, but it makes me angry, too.

I have to go, right away, to my station, where I belong, and where it is empty, and I can settle in for a while with my machine gun, settle, fit myself in it, around it, to it. Like digging in at the batter's box. In a way. But more like digging into a powerful machine gun, I suppose.

I'm not even required to be here for hours yet. Neither are the other guys for that matter. But as far as that goes I wouldn't have left my ship, wouldn't have left my *gun*, not once the entire week, if they hadn't forced me and threatened me with a mental health evaluation. I don't know whether I am a natural fighting man or not. But I knew from the time that first mission ended, and they started picking it all apart, and especially from the moment I heard about what we had lost, I knew with every part of me that I needed nothing so much as I needed to get back up in the air, to have another shot, to get back at least something of what we'd lost.

"I have to go now," I say, illustrating the words by the act of going.

"The A's — it's not your fault," Boyd clarifies, catching me an instant before I've gotten away again. "That they're kinda rotten. That's how they usually are, but I bet you made them better, which is all you can do, really. Right?"

We did. Make them better.

We.

We did. Make that team better. Together.

We did everything together. Better. Everything.

We should have been together. We would be better. The *Yorktown* would have been better, would be better, probably still.

"All the same, though," Boyd says through the stillness that I was both causing and swimming in. "Still, A's will be A's, and I'd bet we could beat that A's team you played for. What, D-ball, right?"

"Yeah, D-ball. Still, only a couple hops up to the majors from there."

"Yeah, I know. But I'm fairly sure we could beat the major league A's, too. So we'd handle you guys without a lot of trouble."

"Dream away, Boyd. I'm going to the nose, get to know the gear again."

"You would be playing for our side, of course," Couley adds.

That pulls me right back in. "Why would I do that?"

"'Cause we're your team now, Theo," Boyd says, stunning me with just the sound of my own old regular-me name.

"What are you up to?" I say to him bluntly.

"I'm just talkin'," he says. "So, go on, you can go. See you around. Nobody here's gonna try and stop you this time."

"Good," I say.

"But don't be a stranger," Boyd calls.

"All right," I call back over my shoulder.

"You know, just come on down this way whenever. Bum around, do nothin', whatever. Have a go on the tail guns, man, you'll love it."

As I get farther away, more volume is required. I don't feel like more volume right now, frankly.

"Top turret, too," Couley adds. "Or the waist guns. Belly gun, as well, since you should really get in some time on every one. In case you have to be drafted in due to an unforeseen circumstance, which is of course entirely foreseeable."

"You mean," I say flatly, as they have managed to draw me back yet again, "like one of us getting killed."

"Yes, precisely," he says with a chilling little swag of pride. "I just heard that air crew are now officially the most likely of all the branches to get shipped home in a box."

"Or not get shipped there at all . . ." I say, because sometimes you know when you're the guy who's supposed to say a thing.

"Yes, of course," he says. "I think the odds they're quoting are like seventy–thirty for each one of us to make it out alive."

"But, hey," Boyd pipes up in a goofy, spirited way, "at least the odds are still falling in our favor."

"Yeah," I say, having heard just about all of the downbeat stuff I can bear for now, "and that ratio has bottomed out. As of now, that percentage of ours is gonna rise steadily, every day, until each man on this crew is on his last and best mission, back to the ZOI." That's zone of interior. That is, home.

Strictly speaking, the gunners, all gunnery trained and qualified to at least sergeant, can rotate to any gun station if all parties agree. I never thought to talk about it with any of the other guys. Mostly because I just about barely talked to them about anything at all, preferring to keep to myself in the isolated cone of glass that is my truest home for however long it lasts.

As I at last reach my small, strange sanctuary, the idea of taking shots from all those positions sends a jolt of excitement through me that even brings back my yell.

"Maybe," I shout. "Maybe. I'll think about it."

If you heard my voice, it would have announced against my wishes that I had already thought about it and the thought suits me mightily.

"The Brotherhood, like it should be," Boyd announces.

I stare from my perch within the greenhouse nose cone. First I peer up into the early-morning sky. Then I stare back in the direction of those two operators, wondering what the operation is costing me.

"What *Brotherhood*?" I demand, appearing in the tail section well before they'd have expected.

"The Brotherhood of Bombardment Squadron Gunners, of course." Couley does a little celebratory full spin of the tail gunner's turret at his pleasure over the whole business — which has obviously sucked me right in.

I note how far we've gone into this discussion together, and how far we'll be treading into Nazi-held territory later today, and the two things together seem like the work of some jokester a lot funnier than I ever was.

I really was the funny one in the family. Seems like a long time ago now.

"Nope," I say, belatedly responding to a provocative moment from some time earlier in the conversation. "Even if you talked me into playing for this hodgepodge of a team, we would never on our best day beat the team I played for in Federalsburg. If we played 'em a hundred times we'd lose a hundred games. I know this, guys. I know baseball, and I know this."

"Well," Couley says, with a big waking-bear stretch before climbing up to his engineer's station. "You definitely sound like a guy who knows. And it's never wise to argue with a guy who knows what he knows and knows it."

"I know that even bad teams often have one great player on them. And one special guy can change a lot of how things can go."

"I guess your team had one of these great players, then?" Couley is speaking from up in his perch. I look at him, then I peek behind me at Boyd faking badly at being absorbed in a bunched up knot of tubes and cables within his gun turret. I turn back to Couley.

"The best, George," I say, with pride leaking out all over me like sap from a maple tree. "Special guy. Great ballplayer, greater man."

He nods at me, proud like he was right in there with me. He knows, of course, though we don't ever talk about it directly. Just like they all know, know everything, before needing to be told.

They are all my brothers after all.

SCARY TO THINK ABOUT. DON'T YOU THINK, HAVING ALL THESE BROTHERS? I FOUND IT SCARY ENOUGH WITH JUST THE ONE.

AS IF THERE WERE NOT MORE THAN ENOUGH SCARY THINGS IN MY HEAD ALREADY, AND I RECKON IN MOST EVERY HEAD WITH A BRAIN INSIDE IT.

BUT THE FIRST TWO MISSIONS ARE BEHIND US AND I CAN SAY THAT I KNOW LESS ABOUT WHAT I'M DOING NOW THAN I DID BEFORE. MISSION ONE, WE WENT IN

WITH A WHOLE BUNCH OF BOMBERS, MET A WHOLE BUNCH OF FIGHTERS, DROPPED LOADS OF BOMBS AND SHOT UP THEIR PLANES JUST LIKE THEY DID TO US. AND IN THE FINAL ANALYSIS YOU HAVE TO SAY THAT A LOT OF THINGS THE NAZIS RELY ON TO KEEP CHURNING OUT THE MACHINERY OF WAR THAT KEEPS THEM IN THE GAME ARE NO LONGER THERE, BECAUSE WE KNOCKED 'EM OUT.

THAT'S A W IN THE WIN COLUMN FOR US, THAT'S WHAT I SAY. BUT IT WAS AS IF WE LOST, BECAUSE WE LOST ONE SINGLE B-17 OUT OF A WHOLE SKY FULL OF BOMBERS. ONE.

I KNOW IT; I HEAR MYSELF. IT WAS TEN GOOD MEN, AND NO MATTER HOW MANY WE BROUGHT BACK HOME WITH US, WE LEFT TEN OF THEM IN THE OCEAN.

HOW DO YOU LIVE WITH THAT KIND OF THING? HUH? TEN IS A LOT, BUT YOU KNEW IT WASN'T GONNA LOOK LIKE MUCH AT ALL, AFTER THE NEXT TRIP OR THE NEXT OR THE NEXT. WHAT THEN? HOW IS A GUY SUPPOSED TO GO ON WITH STATS LIKE THESE HANGING OVER HIM EVERY MORNING HE GETS UP?

THANK GOODNESS FOR BASEBALL IS ALL I CAN REALLY SAY. REMEMBER THAT? YOU REMEMBER, OF COURSE YOU DO, YOU BASHED IT INTO MY HEAD MORE than everybody else put together: It's one of the ways baseball is such a perfect sport, because you don't have a week between games to think too hard about all you messed up. Because there is another game only a day or two later and boy that previous game and whatever, whatever bone-headed play you made, it is in the past and it has to stay there if your head's ever gonna be right. Remember? 'Course ya do, you beat it into my head with your hands almost as much as with the words. Ha. Remember? I remember. Sure you remember.

I remember it all, brother. All of it, all of us. All of you.

But how? How am I supposed to put all this behind me? Every day? By myself?

And what if I can't? Huh? What happens if I can't be strong the way I was supposed to be, the way I thought I was? The way you always were, and still surely are.

Because there wasn't a game the next day for us. How do you like that? No, we had to stew for a week. Then, finally, there was another mission, a big

RAID, LOTS OF STRATEGIC TARGETS HIT, GOOD WORK. ALSO, BY THE WAY, ANOTHER TWO B-17s WENT DOWN, A WHOLE BUNCH MORE WERE PRETTY WELL DAMAGED AND WE ARE STARTING TO BUILD ON OUR CASUALTY SCORES 'CAUSE WE RACKED UP EIGHT OF OUR BOYS WIA. AND, EIGHTEEN MIA.

M, AND I, AND A. THOSE ARE THE WORST, YOU KNOW. THE WORST THREE LETTERS YOU CAN PUT TOGETHER WHEN REPORTING A SERVICEMAN'S STATUS. I TELL YOU WHAT, I THINK I'D RATHER BE A KIA, OR A POW. OR EVEN A DOA. BETTER THAN GOING THROUGH WHATALL BEING SOME KIND OF FOREVER MISSING MIGHT INVOLVE, LIKE MAYBE BEING A GHOST HANGING THERE WITH ONE FOOT IN EACH WORLD BUT ALL THE REAL BUSINESS PARTS OF HIM BEING IN NEITHER. AND, WHILE THAT'S WHAT I THINK I WOULD PREFER IF I WAS THE SERVICEMAN IN QUESTION, AND IF ANYBODY BOTHERED OFFERING ME A CHOICE, AT THE SAME TIME I HAVE NO DOUBT AT ALL HOW I WOULD FEEL IF I WAS THE SURVIVING FAMILY OF THAT POOR SORRY MIA. THE PARENTS, THE BROTHERS, THE SISTERS. 'CAUSE I HAVE SEEN THOSE FACES, BOY. I SEEN 'EM JUST AS LONG AS I COULD STAND TO SEE 'EM BEFORE TURNING AWAY. AND THEN RUNNING AWAY.

Yes. Yes, I know. I should have been better. Better help to them, more comfort. Less of a baby brother and more of a man. Yes. I know. And I know, I have to write them. Though truly, Susan is the writer . . . but yes, yes. I know. I will.

But, I tell you, what I've been wanting to say to you especially, I've been wanting to say that everybody, everybody, every last man wanted to be right in there again after that first raid, like you said, to get in another game as soon as you can, so you can fight and win your way out of it, to beat whatever it was that beat you. Before it had the chance to beat you even more seriously, from inside your own head. The week between was tough, but it ended. For some of the boys, anyway — mostly on the B-17s, because it's frankly becoming obvious that that plane is the teacher's pet of the Eighth Air Force. They got their opportunity to get back in and start punching back.

My bombardment group is the 44th, which in case you're interested, is part of VIII Bomber Command, which is under the "Mighty Eighth

Air Force." Our plane has a name, too, but I'll save you that treat for another day. Anyway, we didn't have that chance to get back in and fight our way back up. Because we were moling, while all that fighting was going on. You know what a mole is, don't you? In the Air Corps, it's a dummy plane, a dummy mission, filled with dummies who don't even know when they take off that they are only flying to some useless no-place just to draw some attention away from the real mission. Which is even worse than being grounded, y'know? Feeling like such big bad heroes on our way up, only to feel that much stupider on the way back.

I could only ever tell you just how crummy I felt returning from that flight.

So, I moled. And I still have not had my second chance, and I just want my chance is all, y'know? I thought I was getting it, too, aw, man you shoulda seen me, boy, thumping my chest like some big dumb crazy flying ape, so excited to get my hands on those rats again. But I was fooled just as bad as the Germans were. And so. And so

THAT'S THAT, I HAVE TO JUST, JUST, WAIT, WAIT FOR TOMORROW'S GAME, RIGHT? RIGHT?

BUT I AIN'T NO MOLE, BROTHER. NO, SIR, I AIN'T NO MOLE OF ANY KIND AND I PLAN TO SHOW 'EM ALL IN A BIG WAY JUST THE FIRST CHANCE I GET. BECAUSE I CAME HERE TO SHOOT MEN DOWN OUT OF THE SKY. AND I'M GONNA BE GREAT AT IT, TOO. YOU'LL SEE. I CAN'T WAIT FOR YOU TO SEE.

SO. RIGHT. ANYWAY. I JUST HAD TO TELL SOMEONE. HAD TO TELL YOU, IS THE THING. I'LL BE ALL RIGHT, THANKS, SO DON'T WORRY ABOUT ME.

OH, AND WE'RE KNOWN AS THE FLYING EIGHT-BALLS, THE 44TH BG. THOUGHT YOU'D LIKE THAT. THERE'LL BE PLENTY MORE TO TELL YOU SOON, TOO, WITHOUT A DOUBT. WHICH IS WHY I WANT YOU TO KEEP ONE OF THESE DIARIES, JUST LIKE THIS ONE I'VE GOT, NOTHING TOO PRISSY. NOT FOR A COUPLE OF MUGS LIKE US WHO CAN HARDLY WRITE.

ANYWAY, SO THAT'S WHAT WE'RE GONNA DO. WE WILL KEEP OUR DIARIES OF OUR EXPERIENCES THROUGH THE WHOLE WAR, AND THEN WHEN IT'S OVER WE WILL HAVE THESE TWO ACCOUNTS, AND WE CAN EXCHANGE THEM. WE'LL COMPARE ALL OUR ADVENTURES AND HORROR

STORIES AND HERO STUFF AND ALL THAT. WE'LL MATCH 'EM UP, RIGHT, AND WE'LL SEE WHO COMES OUT ON TOP. RIGHT? DEAL.

WHO AM I KIDDING? YOU'LL WIN, AND BE CROWNED HERO OF HEROES, 'CAUSE THAT'S THE KIND OF THING YOU ALWAYS DO.

AND HERE'S HOPING YOU DO.

CHAPTER SIX

Does Anybody
See the Light?

Well, no, I don't think it's worthless and embarrassing. Moling is a legitimate part of strategy, and when the strategy works out we are all winning. I don't care if you put me on shoeshine duty, if the shoes are shinin' and the Germans are dyin', then I'm a winner just as much as if I put the bullets into the jerk's face myself."

The speaker is Sergeant Peter Quinn, one of our two regular midship waist gunners. Quinn mans one or the other of the guns that sprout from the B-24's famously broad sides, while Sergeant Billy Hargreaves mans the belly gun, which functions kind of like getting really angry at your downstairs neighbors and trying to shoot them through your floor.

"Yeah, yeah," says Hargreaves, "but which job would you enjoy doing more?"

"What?" says Quinn. "Don't be simple, Billy. If they

let me have my way, the whole bunch of us would have no guns. We'd —"

"Waaa-haaa . . ." All five of us at once cut him off, howling laughter because of the crazy non-Quinn-ness of the very idea of disarmament.

"Hey hey hey, if you'll allow a guy to finish . . . I was gonna say that if I could make it happen then everybody would just be issued with bullets and hammers. We'd have to hunt and chase each other down, get the other guy onto the ground, and, *pow*, hammer the bullet right into the guy's skull. Huh? What an idea, huh? Fairer every way you look at it. You'd have to be tough, and fit, and you'd have to have the stomach to say hello right to the ugly mug of your enemy before making brainburgers out of him. No more of this wishy-wash of killin' folk from a million miles away. The better man would *always win*." He smiles but still doesn't pause for a breath. "Killing the enemy with more fairness *and* more fun. Tell me now, beautiful or beautiful?"

It's always pretty much like that when Quinn speaks. Nobody knows where he gets it. But he shows no sign of ever running out of it.

And I, for one, am glad. When he goes off on one of those runs, I go right along with him. There is more fun, more noise, more . . . distraction that comes with that stuff. Keeps a guy in the spirit, and in the group, and out of the dangerous dark corners of his own head.

This hammer-and-bullets debate is just the latest in a growing collection of daffy conversations among us. Us, being — incredibly, to my mind — the very Brotherhood that Boyd boldly predicted we would become. Sergeant Henry "Hank" Boyd, no less. I am not going to call him Hank, not now and not ever. But I am going to admit that this thing, this tight-knit knot of nuts who have a lot in common despite being nothing alike beyond us all being sergeants and all being gunners, has quickly become the Brotherhood that was foretold to me. Or should that be, forewarned? And I didn't even want one more brother.

"Beautiful?" Dodge says to him in an upswinging, theatrical voice that sounds like he had to have acted in a school play at some point. "Well, yeah, I suppose it's a *kind* of beautiful." He's a ham, but he's also a good teammate, and when conditions call for the pilot to order Dodge down from his comfy radio-man's perch and man his gun, the three of them, Quinn, Hargreaves, and Dodge, could not be a more perfect left-center-right trio of midsection gunners. They don't stop yelling crazy-boasty-threatening stuff — to each other or to the Messerschmitts trying to put big fat bullet holes in all of us. They scream blood and guts through every last shot of a firefight, and in my opinion it's one of the things that makes this team, under pressure, the most fearsome and determined bunch I have ever been around. We *change* from the instant we start getting shot at. We *improve*, if it's okay to say that. Even if it's not okay to say it, I'm saying it.

And those three, sticking out either side of the Batboy's rib section and out of his belly button, are even more of a team than the rest of us. Because the two are like the left and the right side of one big dope of a person while the third is, I guess, the hard abdominal center.

And I'm certain they have no idea how lucky they are with that.

We are all just getting up from the table, from breakfast, in the mess, which is a *mess*, no matter how much they clean it. We're getting up together because we do everything together, whether we like it or not.

Each one of the six of us would tell you *not*. And each one of the six of us would be lying. We've been cooped up together, almost twenty-four hours a day, since we plunked down in Shipdham not even a month ago. If we aren't doing our business in the cramped and freezing, earsplitting, and bone-rattling B-24, then we are likewise huddled like a den of badgers in the newly built living quarters the RAF has provided just for the lucky men of the USAAF. More honestly, the facilities seem like they were newly built for the fighters of the *previous* Great World War or whatever they called it, or possibly for the Great One before that. The only thing that's for sure is that the place we currently call home makes us yearn for the comforts of the aircraft.

We complain loudly about the living conditions, the weather, the food, the officers, the assignments, the boredom, and anything else that we can think of, which doesn't take much thinking power. But most of all, we complain about each other, so relentlessly that any outside observer would be amazed that all six of us are highly trained gunnery school graduates handling high-powered weapons every day and not one of us has shot any of the others. Yet.

"Okay," Boyd pipes up as we cross the field and approach the waiting and ready Batboy. "I'm sold, Sarge. It's a beautiful idea."

"Yeah," I say, "the kind of beauty you don't run into every day, unless you live in a maximum-security prison, I suppose."

"Wouldja listen to Ol' Sergeant Sunshine over there," Dodge calls out. "Remember, Rosie Nosegun, I'm the official listener up there in my radio observatory seat when I'm not too busy giving them rotten German birds a little buckshot. And from what I can hear outta your direction, I could make quite a recording of what comes out of *your* mouth once the shootin' starts."

I have no idea what he is referring to. I honestly don't.

"Ah, man, Dodge, you're just making stuff up now."

"Ha!" he yells. "You really don't know, do ya? Even nuttier than I thought there, bats-in-the-belfry boy. I for sure have to see if I can get you recorded. And then you better be nicer to me, 'cause I'm pretty sure if I sent the evidence off to the Geneva Convention folks or whoever, you could already be up for war crimes based on your mouth alone."

From the way every other guy is laughing and pointing in my direction, I'm afraid I can neither defend myself nor completely rule out his possible truthfulness.

That should be worrying, I guess.

Guys are slapping my back and pushing me along a kind of instant honor-guard lineup as I approach the entrance to the plane. We've developed this kind of semiofficial routine, where we enter in order of distance from the opening. So, Rosie Nosegun gets first go.

"Thank you, thank you," I say, bowing and waving as each back smack gets harder, then the odd kick gets in.

It goes like this now. The closer we get to the hour, the closer we get to the plane, to the air and the target and the enemy action, the more mania we can feel bubbling up among us.

In a slight disruption of protocol, Couley slips in behind me ahead of Dodge. He bumps me pretty hard, knocking me forward just as I step on the narrow plank of the walkway.

"Hey, easy, man," I say, and I hear nothing in return. This is unusual and makes me realize that I don't think I have heard him speak a word yet today. When we get to the point where he is to mount his engineer's station and I am to continue onto the nose where I will trade elbows with the officer grade of knucklehead for a while, I stop. I grab hold of Couley's arm before he can climb up into his seat. "What's wrong with you today? You all right?"

For a couple of seconds he just stares, like he's giving thought to whether or not he's even going to respond. Eventually he decides he will.

"What are we doing here, Theo?"

My turn to stare. "That? That's your answer to my question of what's bothering you? Another question? A question, I might add, that could take some time to answer in any meaningful way."

"I mean, come on, what are we doing going after U-boats in open water? We're not built for that. There are actually other craft that are specifically tailored to that."

"I'm sure they'll be there, too."

He just shakes his head a lot for a bit, then pats me hard on the shoulder. "Never mind. I'm just shooting off my mouth. Bad mood I guess."

"Okay, guy," I say and punch his shoulder twice as hard before stepping toward my nose gun.

"I just seem to have these moods come over me, you know, strangely enough, every time it occurs to me that the people running the Mighty Eighth Air Force do not know what they are doing, here in the European Theater of Operations and as a result we are all, each and every one of us in his turn, going to die in a really gruesome, fiery way because of them."

I stop short and execute easily the crispest pinpoint toe-heel about-face since basic training. I find Couley already settled into his station. And, I should add, looking so poised and professional that it's spooky. It hardly seems possible the words that caught me from behind came out of the face that's regarding me now.

"Jeez, Couley, and to think somebody just called *me* Sergeant Sunshine. Nice pep talk there, boy."

He shows almost no facial reaction to me, but when he speaks again, he smiles. "Just do me a favor, will ya?

Just to be on the safe side and leave nothing to chance or to the Bomber Command head-scratchers, I'd sure feel a whole lot better if you would kill, oh, everybody out there today. Just kill lots and lots of Germans. 'Cause I do have faith in you, kid. Wouldja do that for me?"

I give him a salute, just so that we both can see how cockamamie this exchange actually is, and say, "I'm honored. That means a lot to me, even if you are, y'know, nuts. But who cares, right? I don't. So, consider 'em all dead, pal."

He's smiling broadly as I go, and I am determined once and for all to get to my station, no matter what else I might hear. And that determination comes in good and handy when I hear just this little bit more.

"I do, now. I consider them all dead. I'm looking forward to it being official. I'm a great admirer of your work."

I all but nose-dive into the nose cone just to get to a place where I think I understand how everything is supposed to function, and can rely on it all to make the same sense it did yesterday.

Everybody at one time or another says that all of us airmen are at least a little insane. And everybody means it to a different degree, and with a variety of different interpretations of insanity.

That's all on that subject for now. There's work ahead.

"What are we trying to prove with this stuff anyway, huh?" Gallagher says instead of hello, confirming that there is something in the air today that's making guys act funny, which is giving me a feeling that is anything but.

"Well," I say, "since I don't really quite get the nature of the question and I have no desire to ask you to clarify it, I'm just gonna take a shot and say we're trying to prove that the Armed Forces of the United States of America are the equal or better of anyone else's on earth, and that we can lead the world as a moral force for good, opposing tyranny of all kinds. And if we put enough planes in the air and drop enough bombs then that will settle matters so everybody can go home and live peacefully."

I am not proud of how easily I seem to be able to ruffle Gallagher's feathers, or of how frequently I enjoy doing it. But, I'm not not proud of it, either.

"What?" he blurts. "What are you talking about? I mean this whole daylight raid business. Broad-daylight bombing with almost no fighter escort cover at all. I don't like it. The Brits and Germans have already been at it over here for what, three years? And they *both* decided it was a demented idea and switched to night bombing rather than have their planes *and their crews* falling out of the sky so quickly they might as well have just saved the fuel, kept them on the runways, and shot all their own guys instead."

While I am absorbing this rant that has been obviously growing like a gas ball in Gallagher's stomach — though less obvious is why he was saving it for me — I find myself giving every vital element of my trusted machine gun an extra-diligent going-over. It seems like people here are suddenly getting all inquisitive about the very basic whatall at the core of what we shooter-bomber-flyer operations are achieving. And, sure, that's fine. They can do that. Maybe the way we are going about our mission to rid the world of evil isn't perfect, and speaking up and questioning might improve things in the future. You can't take much for granted, because we sure are seeing the machinery of warfare changing almost by the day with all these countries competing to match and mimic and surpass one another's newest, fastest, blastiest explosive devices and the systems that deliver them. So maybe there's room for helpful criticism from a bombardier. Like I said, maybe it'll amount to something in the future. Good luck with that.

But me, I've been thinking an awful lot lately. And by that I mean filling every second of every day that isn't bombarded with the noise and chatter and boom and bam of activity that makes up this life I'm in, filling all those seconds with a different sort of thought about the future. And that thought is: I don't know whether there's any such thing. I'm not at all sure I even have much of what you'd call a future stretching out in front of me. All those idle seconds, that's the thought that's wedging itself in my brain when the noise stops, unless I'm sleeping. Actually, no, the sleeping part isn't true anymore, I forgot. I do wish there was more of the noise and chatter and boom and bam.

All doubts about the future aside, I am mostly certain that I have got a *right now*, and my right now is fast and ferocious and happening at the very front tip of one of the truest sky monsters of all time. All of my sky time has to be considered hot action time, even while it is cold like frostbite.

So what I mean is, I have now, and I have this, and while that is the case I can only do my best and be prepared and be right at the top of my game because these German boys sure seem to be exactly that.

I have to kill people. I have to try my hardest and kill as many of those people as I can manage. I understand, that they are also trying to kill me. People I have never met want to kill me. I still stagger a little bit over that one at least once per day when it pops up the reliable way it does. They *really* want to kill me, I can see how much because from where I work, I *see* many of these faces.

And I really want to kill them, preferably, y'know, first.

Can they see it in my face? Do those guys see me too?

"You're not even listening to me, are you?" Gallagher says.

"Yes, I am," I say, because luckily I caught the question part there just in time. "But I'm also oiling my machine gun and making sure the armaments guys didn't leave me short of rounds like they did once before and which, I tell you what, they will never do to me again."

"Also," Lieutenant Bell jumps in, "he's not listening to you because the kid is learning fast that you are full of bologna."

Whoa. The day is picking up already and we haven't even started the engines yet.

Buuuu-buuu-buuu-buuuwhaaaarrrr . . .

And now we have engines.

"What are you talking about, Bell?" Gallagher asks defensively.

"I'm talking about you," Bell snaps back. He is sounding grouchier than usual, and right now I'm starting to wonder why I didn't like him more from the start. "And I'm talking about the mission, this mission, all the missions. There are only two groups of B-24s in the Eighth Air Force. *Two!* There's gonna be more eventually, but right now, we are it. So unless we want the insufferable B-17 groups to do everything —"

"No, we don't!" I blurt.

"Of course not. So, they tell us to go someplace and bomb something, then we go to that place and we bomb that thing. What do we care, as long as we're productively destroying stuff?"

Productively destroying stuff. Constructive destruction. I think I have a new favorite job description.

"Yeah," Gallagher says, "but how productive is it if we drop out of the sky before we get to the *destroying stuff* part? In case you haven't noticed, bomber groups in the European Theater are starting to lose planes — and crews — at a scary rate."

"Ah," Lieutenant Bell says, sounding a lot like a guy who's just won at something. He's turned away from the nose and the glass and Gallagher to address his navigator's table. I've seen him do this a number of times now when he wants to send a message of contempt to somebody. Having been that somebody more than once already, I can testify to the almost irresistible urge to punch the back of that head as soon as he shows it to you. Now, as I keep one eye on our bombardier's darkening purple face, I'm thinking the back of Bell's head is not such an awful thing.

"What do you mean by 'Ah'?"

"I mean," Bell says to his table, which I can see clearly in my mind even with him behind me, "ah, I was wondering which thing scared you the most about the daytime bombings, whether it was the danger or the fact that daytime bombing obviously requires a lot more skill from the bombardier. But, now I know that it's more the fighters you're afraid of, and less about your accuracy problems. . . ."

"Well why *don't* we have our own fighter escort, it doesn't make . . . wait, 'accuracy problems'?"

We are taxiing now, falling into the flight line with our squadron in the middle of the two others assigned to the mission.

"Well, not problems, as such. But you're getting the shakes about having to aim at a big ol' U-boat, and not in open water either, since we are headed right up to their pens. And we hear it all the time about these amazing bombardiers who can hit a tuna in the middle of the ocean from ten thousand feet. Mostly the eagle-eye guys on the *Fortresses*, of course . . ."

"Of course," I spit. It really is easy to hate the Flying Fortress guys. "They never shut up about how great they are. And anyway, why would a fortress fly, huh? It makes no sense. A fortress is like a castle or a bunker or something that's solid and dug in and the opposite of flying."

My contribution to the debate gets a little lost as we hit our spot and roar our engines and in a few seconds get airborne and on our way to some construc-tive destruction.

"Tell you what, Mr. Navigator," Gallagher says, down and staring through his sights already like he can force it all to come to him right away. "How 'bout you just agree to get us to the IP without your usual zigzags and curlicues, and then I will nail you so much tuna it'll be tuna salad raining down from the sky and coming out your nose for a month, okay?"

Disgusting as that wound up at the end there, Gallagher's readiness is a good thing. The IP is the initial penetration point, the spot where the bomb run officially begins about eighteen-to-twenty miles from the target destination. It's when control of the aircraft falls from the pilot to the bombardier, making it his show to get us on top of our intended victim. The IP is also the point beyond which standing orders for all bomber missions get extra specific, serious, and maybe a little nerve-wracking if you think about it too much. Every aircraft that makes it past the IP is forbidden to diverge from the course that was laid out at the morning briefing. *No evasive maneuvers permitted.* Up till then, we would make any number of wide S turns to evade danger — or *zigzags and curlicues*, as Gallagher would put it — but for the last stretch, boys, you drive straight for that target and you just gotta put up your dukes and fight whoever and whatever wants to come and have some.

And it's only now, as I'm thinking about it, that I remember again how this is the most thrilling and exciting and, yeah, *magical* part of my day. You would think a guy wouldn't need to be reminded of a feeling like that, but I do. Great as it is as it's happening, it's like a blackout thing, where the memory keeps separating itself from me afterwards.

"Don't worry, gentlemen," I say, swiveling my center machine gun up and down and then jumping on the left cheek gun and then the right cheek gun like I'm some combination of Old West shootist and circus acrobat. "I am in an extra killing mood today so you all can just go about your business and not even look up from your calculations, 'cause I got you covered."

No question about it, there is a higher level of true aggressive menace swirling around this aircraft today than anything I have felt before. It's very special.

"Well, ah, all right, then. Thank you, Sergeant," says a surprised-but-pleased-sounding Lieutenant Bell.

"Yeah, so?" says a predictably jerky and kickable Lieutenant Gallagher. "So, what you're announcing is, basically, that you are gonna do your job. Peachy. Swell. Will you be wanting extra pay for that, too?"

Oh, man. Never mind extra pay, I'd work the whole next month for free if they'd just let me shoot him once the mission is completed.

"That would be very nice, Lieutenant Gallagher," I say, making the rounds of my guns even more slickly and lightning fast than the last time.

I swear, even if we get lost, or the enemy gets smart and doesn't show up to oppose us, I think we'll all start firing these weapons up here today anyway, because we gotta get it out somehow.

It's making me nostalgic for my old baseball days, which hasn't happened in a while. A great big benches-clearing Donnybrook would be just the thing now.

Except.

Hank had always watched my back. In every single last brawl.

He sure can't do it now. Instead, I'm heading into a fight with *eight* highly trained combat specialists lined up at my back, in every sense, and one warplane after another of similar gangs aligned behind them.

Not that I don't have faith in this force right here, because I do, but I'd trade the entire Mighty Eighth AF to have Hank behind me instead.

Our target turns out to be Saint-Nazaire, which comes as very little surprise since the port at Saint-Nazaire has been a legendary enough place for a lot of reasons throughout the whole war. It's a major repair operation with a massive dry dock and the only one big enough to handle the Nazis' biggest sea monsters like the battleships *Bismarck* and *Tirpitz*. It had also been the main staging area for the brutal U-boat attacks on merchant shipping, convoys, and the Liberty ships that the United States had been sending across to try and help out the Brits well before we were technically involved in the war. Saint-Nazaire was the source of all those nasty sneaky subs that had been prowling under the waters of New York's outer harbor, and the Carolinas' and Florida's so far back most Americans were barely aware at the time of any serious conflict being carried on in

Europe, and the few who noticed were not really concerned. That's what the papers were all saying anyway, after everything blew up in our faces and the Japanese bombed another famous harbor that I still can't bring myself to name out loud.

WHILE AMERICA SLEPT! is basically what all the big newspapers said when we were humiliated by a sucker punch way off in the Pacific, which changed every aspect of life in America and eventually most other places in the world, too. In the span of less than two hours and with more than two thousand murders, Japan stepped right up, jumped onto the front pages, and made itself the bully of everybody's nightmares. It was the kind of low-down, dirty move that would cost a local guy every friend he had, and on a bigger scale forced just about every country in the world to fall one way or the other. One way to react was, hey, I don't want any trouble and looking down at your shoelaces. The other way, taken by most nations with at least a granule of actual human soul among their leaders, was to condemn this inexcusable act without reservation.

Oh, right, there was a third way. Four days later and

over seven thousand miles away, Germany declared war on the United States.

My brother passed through that famous harbor in the sunny Pacific paradise more than once. He loved it instantly and couldn't wait to tell me all about what made the place so special. He put it all in a letter.

I read it a lot, still. Last letter I got from him. Most recent, anyway.

Anyway, the point of all this is the whole interconnectedness of everything now. The full circleness. It was always there, of course. The Earth is round, after all. But we keep seeing it now, keep knowing it, because this gigantic miserable war connects everything to everything eventually. And this gives the newspapers all those great opportunities to connect the dots and sketch the maps and shout the headlines that connect the far-flung nasty places like Japan and Germany by way of a few other nasty places like Bulgaria and Italy but even more by way of the *quiet bystander nations who stood by and did nothing!* Kind of like *while America slept!*

Just as, it seems, these same newspapers who are shouting at everybody now were napping the whole time German submarines were slithering just as they pleased like monstrous steel eels up and down the east coast of America. They sulked from New York — where those shouty newspapers probably could have seen them from their office windows — to Florida, with my folks place in Maryland right there in between. Which is funny in that way that awful things are funny because the very week I fled the house in Accokeek and ran back to the war, didn't German subs deliver saboteurs *all the way right up to American shores* in both New York and Florida right under everybody's noses? Right under my very flight path to England, probably, just to make one more point about the full circleness of everything now.

And those subs made it all that way and threatened our very soil and my very family after launching from the base at Saint-Nazaire.

"It's mine now, boys, all mine!" Gallagher screams like a maniac the instant we cross the IP. The air all around is popping, both inside the Batboy and out, as the whole crew screams murder and tries to deliver it, while ME-109s and FW-190s swarm us from more angles than even seem possible, peppering every sight line with streams of rounds that appear to have no end. I feel us getting hit, often and all over but that is almost a sideshow because we are also learning the hard way why Saint-Nazaire has the nickname "Flak City." The air is thick and noxious as the famous German antiaircraft shells sweep and arc and then explode, timed precisely to do their dirty business when they reach our bombing altitude.

An altitude, which at about eighteen thousand feet, is seven thousand lower than we would choose to drop from. The B-24 is renowned for many things, and high-altitude bombing is one of them. So we should be higher. This feels very much like we are playing somebody else's game, in their home ballpark.

The two groups of B-17s we linked up with are ahead of us and another several thousand feet lower still. There is no doubt those boys are absorbing a lot of punishment, a lot of damage to both machinery and personnel.

It is chaos, from the moment we get close enough to draw their fighters. The flak assault is relentless, and only getting faster, bigger, louder as we bear down on the targets. I get knocked completely sideways and off my feet by a shell that doesn't even hit us but detonates so close by that it rumbles every bolt holding the Liberator together. I land on a highly focused bombardier, who screams without words, torques like a sidewinder, and punches me crisply on the cheek.

It doesn't hurt or shock me or even register as a real thing in the midst of everything else happening all around that is already so much bigger than life and scarier than death. I jump to my feet and jump back on my gun, banging shoulders with Bell who is manning the gun to my left. He doesn't seem to notice me at all as he beams in on a Messerschmitt wheeling right for us, or right for Bell, to be more specific, as the fighter pilot fishtails a sharp turn that looks like it's going to end right here in the glasshouse with us.

But Bell locks onto the German before he can lock onto Bell, and I swing over and pour everything I have into joining Bell's barrage, pummeling the cockpit glass and the face that is no longer a face, no longer a head, no longer a recognizably human anything. The pilot fairly explodes, with the blood and mush of him filling the cockpit before splashing out of it every which way.

And we are one lucky Liberator as the Messerschmitt looks so certain to hit us head-on that I actually jump backward just in time to watch the full finale as the flaming plane snaps down violently, straight toward the ground, like a big nasty dog getting its snout slapped down by its master.

It's impossible to decide whether we are the aggressor or the target once we feel the disorientation at the very center of this man-made storm. Somehow we have made it over the submarine docking bays. The U-boats are all visible below.

Some kind of distantly human screech comes out of Gallagher just as we feel the thwump of the bomb bay doors opening and the glorious whistle song of the full payload of bombs. All the other smoke and boom shrinks away into total feebleness in the wake of our Armageddon of rapid-sequence bomb blasts that shake the sky as much as the earth. And it's a whole new experience from this low altitude. We can actually feel the heat of our success blast right up back to us, and something even more incredible and victorious and sickening rides up with it. I am certain that I'm smelling the flash burning of human flesh, wafting through the very same bomb bay doors that delivered those men their death. It's as if they just had to fly up and force us to breathe in the thing we did. To get it right up into us, into our sinuses and our pores as we make our sweeping, banking turn back to home where it will linger, and rot, and stay with us always. I am quite sure of that.

I am already queasy thinking about it when, behind me, from just beyond the pilot's deck, I hear a violence of vomiting that does not help things at all.

CHAPTER SEVEN

I Tell You What

ARE YOU KEEPING UP? WITH THE DIARY, ARE YOU KEEPING UP WITH YOUR ENTRIES LIKE I TOLD YOU TO? BECAUSE IF NOT, AND AT THE END OF THE WAR THE MOVIE PEOPLE HAVE MOSTLY MY WRITING TO WORK FROM, DON'T COME CRYING TO ME WHEN YOU LOOK LIKE A BIT PLAYER WITH SOMEBODY LIKE MAYBE MICKEY ROONEY AS HENRY McCALLUM WHILE I'M BEING PLAYED BY JIMMY STEWART. HE'S ONE OF US, YOU KNOW. ARMY AIR CORPS AND A QUALIFIED BOMBER PILOT, NO LESS. I KNOW ALL THE HOLLYWOOD GUYS ARE JUST PLAYING DRESS-UP AND MAKING RECRUITMENT FILMS, BUT THERE ARE STRONG RUMORS CIRCULATING THAT HE'S GETTING HIMSELF SENT OVER HERE, AS A REAL PILOT IN A REAL EIGHTH AIR FORCE BOMBARDMENT GROUP. MAKES SENSE THOUGH, RIGHT? HOW'S HE SUPPOSED TO PLAY ME RIGHT IF HE DOESN'T COME OVER AND WATCH ME IN ACTION?

AND OH, BROTHER, HAVE I BEEN IN ACTION.

To tell you the truth, I don't know if you are going to be getting equal screen time even if you do write your stories down. I'll admit, having your aircraft carrier basically destroyed TWICE and surviving BOTH times...that does probably give you a bit of a head start. But it won't be enough if I keep going the way I'm going right now, I'll tell you what.

You know I'm a nose gunner on a B-24 Liberator heavy bomber, right? And now I'll tell you, the guys named the thing after me. You know, the way they do with the planes, decorating the noses and all? Well, the kid they painted up there doesn't look like me, but he is carrying a bat and dressed almost sort of like a baseball player. And the name of the thing, and, yeah, go ahead and laugh, because you're you, right? I wouldn't want to tell you not to laugh. 'Cause I like the sound of your laugh, always did, remember? Even when you were laughing at me, which was most of the time. Whatever it is in your laugh, I couldn't help myself, even if you were standing on my head in the dirt and I was crying, all of a sudden I was

LAUGHING, TOO. LAUGHING MY HEAD OFF I WOULD HAVE SAID, IF YOU WEREN'T KEEPING MY HEAD FIRMLY IN PLACE. BECAUSE YOU WERE STANDING ON IT.

REMEMBER THAT, HANK?

AW, NOW LOOK. YOU GOT ME ALL BOTHERED AND EVERYTHING AND, MAN, I COULD USE A LAUGH, I REALLY COULD. I'D BE ALL RIGHT IF YOU COULD JUST SEND ME ONE FROM WHEREVER IT IS YOU'RE HIDING. AND IF I COULD JUST HEAR IT, JUST CATCH THAT SLOW ROLLING RUMBLE OF YOURS FOR EVEN A FEW SECONDS, I THINK I'D GET A BOOST AND STOP GETTING ALL WEAK AND BOTHERED HERE. I CAN'T BE LIKE THAT, AS I'M SURE YOU KNOW ALREADY I'M A GUNNER, MISTER, AND I'M HARD AS NAILS AT IT, I REALLY AM. SO, IF I CAN'T CONVINCE YOU TO THROW A LAUGH MY WAY, I'LL JUST HAVE TO CHEER MYSELF THE WAY I DO THESE DAYS. I'LL GO OUT AND KILL SOME PEOPLE NEXT TIME I FLY. THAT SEEMS TO CHEER ME UP A WHOLE LOT.

KILLED A GUY JUST THE OTHER DAY, IN FACT. SHARED HIM, REALLY, WITH A NAVIGATOR, LIEUTENANT BELL, WHO DOUBLES AS A GUNNER BESIDE ME IN THE NOSE CONE WHEN THINGS GET HEAVY, EVEN THOUGH IT'S CRAMPED ENOUGH ALREADY AND I CAN HANDLE THREE GUNS BY

MYSELF, THANKS ALL THE SAME. BUT, I AM A TEAM
PLAYER, RIGHT, YOU'D KNOW THAT BETTER THAN ANYBODY,
SO WE TWO GUNNERS GUNNED, ALL RELENTLESS, STRAIGHT
INTO THE FACE OF THIS MESSERSCHMITT THAT LOOKED
FOR ALL THE WORLD LIKE HE WAS INTENDING TO
SMASH RIGHT INTO MY VERY COMPARTMENT. I'LL TELL
YOU WHAT, BY THE TIME YOU TALLIED IT UP I WOULD
SAY LIEUTENANT BELL AND I HAD POURED A GOOD
TWENTY OR THIRTY POUNDS OF .50-CALIBER ROUNDS
INTO THAT SQUARE GERMAN FACE OF HIS, MAKING FOR
ONE HEAVY HEAD FOR THE LAST FEW SECONDS HE ACTU-
ALLY HAD ONE. WE SAW THE THING EXPLODE, HANK, NO
BIT OF A LIE.

REMEMBER THAT THING WITH THE FROG AND THE
FIRECRACKERS? WELL MULTIPLY THAT BY ABOUT A THOU-
SAND AND THERE YOU HAVE IT.

THAT PART I'LL WANT IN THE MOVIE. I WAS JUST
THINKING, I DON'T WANT THAT OTHER STUFF, ALL THAT
CORN ABOUT WHAT I THINK ABOUT YOUR LAUGH, TO BE
PUT IN THE MOVIE. NOT QUITE SURE YET ABOUT THE
STANDING ON MY HEAD THING, BUT THERE'S STILL TIME,
SO, WE'LL LEAVE THAT FOR NOW.

So, except for the endless parade of German fighters chasing us and trying to kill us all the time (and by the way, I don't know how much of a handful those Japanese flyers have been, but I'm here to tell you that these German boys are every bit as good as advertised. Maybe even better, because before I saw for myself, I couldn't have imagined the things they can do with them planes and not to mention that they do the whole flying and shooting show to make our bomber lives every which way a misery WHILE at the same time weaving and dancing between the solar system of flak that is sent up by their own side and could kill their own guys just as easily as us) I could swear we were at war with France, since that's the place we've been kicking the snot out of mostly. I don't know, man, I think by the time we "liberate" them some more and offer them their country back, they just might decide to say no thanks. I could understand, sort of, but then I would want to say back to them, well, if you really liked the place the way it was you might have thought about giving

THE NAZIS A LITTLE HARDER TIME TAKING IT AWAY FROM YOU. THERE WERE STILL A LOT OF LOW MILEAGE FRENCH TANKS SITTING AROUND JUST LOOKING PRETTY FROM WHAT I'VE HEARD.

I HATE THE FLAK, MAN, I REALLY DO.

ANYWAY, YOU KNOW HOW THEY SAY ALL COMBAT AIR CREW ARE AT LEAST A LITTLE BIT CRAZY? WELL THEY DO, AND I FIND THAT IT'S REALLY DIFFICULT TO TELL, BECAUSE IT'S LIKE A RELATIVE THING — AND, NO, I HEAR YOU LAUGHING NOW BUT I DON'T MEAN A RELATIVE LIKE UNCLE HAMISH WITH THE PANTS AND THE TEETH AND THE THING — I MEAN MORE LIKE RELATIVE TO ALL THE GUYS YOU SEE AROUND YOU, IN THE SAME PREDICAMENTS, THE SAME TIGHT SPACES, FACING THE SAME THREATS AND DOING THE THINGS YOU HAVE TO DO AND SEEING THE THINGS YOU HAVE TO SEE OTHER PEOPLE DO, AND THEN THERE'S THE FOOD AND EVERYTHING ELSE. YOU GOTTA COMPARE TO YOUR PEOPLE, NOW DON'T YOU? WELL, THESE ARE MY PEOPLE NOW AND — I'M NOT LOONY SO DON'T THINK IT — WHEN I LOOK AROUND, SNEAK A PEEK OVER MY SHOULDER DOWN TOWARD THE BOMB-SIGHTING STATION ON THE FLOOR NEAR MY FEET, WELL I DON'T KNOW WHAT TO THINK WHEN I TRY TO MEASURE UP WITH

MY PEOPLE HERE. I DON'T KNOW HOW I MEASURE, IS AS CLOSE AS I CAN COME TO TELLING YOU.

WHEN YOU WERE MY PEOPLE, BOY I ALWAYS, ALWAYS KNEW WHO I WAS, AND I WAS ABSOLUTELY FINE WITH THAT KNOWLEDGE AND THAT WHO.

SO HERE I WENT FROM SORT OF KEEPING TO MYSELF AT FIRST, THEN GETTING KIND OF PALLY WITH THE GUYS WHO FELT MOST LIKE MY GUYS, ALL OF THEM GUNNERS AND ALL OF THEM SERGEANTS AND PRETTY ALL RIGHT GUYS WHO MIGHT ALSO BE VARIOUS GRADES OF NUTTY, BUT I LOST MY ABILITY TO TELL THAT KIND OF THING.

EXCEPT WITH THE OFFICERS, OF COURSE, WHO I DON'T ENGAGE WITH ANY MORE THAN NECESSARY, AND ONE OF WHICH I AM GOING TO MAYBE, MAYBE, HAVE TO DO A BODILY HARM BEFORE THIS THING IS OVER.

THE KILL I SHARED WAS OVER A SUBMARINE INSTALLATION WE WERE BOMBING FROM A LEVEL WE WERE NOT USED TO AND NOT SUITED TO. THE B-24 IS A BURLY, BULKY BIRD AND PROBABLY THE ONE ADVANTAGE THAT THE FAMOUS FLYING FOOTREST THAT IS THE B-17 HAS OVER US IS GREATER MANEUVERABILITY, ESPECIALLY AT LOWER LEVELS AND IN THE FORMATIONS THAT BOMBER GROUPS

HAVE TO HOLD LIKE OUR LIVES DEPEND ON IT BECAUSE OUR LIVES VERY MUCH DO. I WORRY SOMETIMES. ESPECIALLY AFTER I'VE BEEN TALKING WITH OUR ENGINEER, COULEY, WHO IS ALSO TOP TURRET GUNNER AND A SERGEANT AND SO MOSTLY ALL RIGHT. BUT HE HAS SOMETHING LIKE AN OBSESSION WITH THE WEAK POINTS AND FLAWS AND — THIS IS THE REALLY GREAT PART — WHAT HE CALLS THE "TRAGEDY-IN-WAITING QUALITIES" OF THE WHOLE FLEET OF LIBERATORS. NOW, AM I WRONG? AM I OVERSENSITIVE OR SOMETHING, OR IS THAT KIND OF UNHELPFUL STUFF TO BE SAYING?

SURE, I CAN TAKE IT, BUT A LOT OF GUYS ON A CREW LIKE OURS MIGHT NOT BE HANK McCALLUM'S BROTHER, RIGHT, YOU KNOW? THEY MIGHT BE MADE OF SOFTER STUFF THAT WON'T ABSORB WHAT HANK McCALLUM'S BROTHER WAS TAUGHT TO SHRUG OFF EVERY DAY OF HIS LIFE.

ANYWAY, THERE ARE FLAWS. THEY ARE REAL, BUT SO WHAT, AND WHAT'S THE USE OF THINKING ABOUT THEM ALL THE TIME? I LOVE THAT PLANE SO MUCH I WISH THEY WOULD LET ME TAKE IT HOME TO ACCOKEEK WITH ME WHEN WE'RE DONE FIXING THINGS FOR EVERYBODY OVER HERE. IT DOESN'T BELLY-LAND VERY WELL, APPARENTLY, IN

AN EMERGENCY. THERE ARE LEAKS. LIKE AIR COMES INSIDE THE FUSELAGE THROUGH SMALL UNSEALED SEAMS. AND AT TWENTY-FIVE THOUSAND FEET IT IS VERY UNWELCOME AIR. AND GAS, A LOT OF TIMES, LEAKS OUT. VERY ODD SETUP WITH THE DISTRIBUTION OF GAS TANKS ALL OVER THE STRUCTURE, INCLUDING THROUGH PARTS OF OUR WINGS. DAVIS WINGS, MOUNTED REAL HIGH AND THIN, WHICH IS WHY WE CAN GO SO MUCH FASTER AND FARTHER WHILE CARRYING MORE TONNAGE THAN THE B-17 EVERYBODY LOVES SO MUCH. IT'S A BEAUTIFUL DESIGN, OUR WING. BUT THERE'S TALK THAT MAYBE YOU DON'T WANT TO BUMP TOO HARD A LANDING UNDER THEM. BUT TALK, RIGHT? THE ARMY RUNS ON TALK, ISN'T THAT WHAT THEY SAY? SO THEN THE ARMY AIR CORPS MUST RUN ON HIGHER TALK EVEN, HUH?

THING IS, HANK, THOSE FLYING FORTRESS GUYS, WE'VE WORKED WITH THEM A LOT AND THEY ARE REALLY OKAY. THEY JUST ENJOY A LITTLE BIT OF RAZZING THE OTHER TEAM IS ALL, AND, HEY, WAS ANYBODY EVER ANY BETTER THAN THE McCALLUM BROTHERS AT THAT? NO. SO MOSTLY, FROM WHAT I CAN TELL, THEY'RE A-OK GUYS.

THE B-17S, WHEN WE FLEW THAT LOW-LEVEL MISSION OVER THE SUBMARINE BASE, WELL, THEY HAD TO FLY EVEN

LOWER. AND, WELL ANYWAY, THEY GOT KIND OF MAULED, IS WHAT HAPPENED, HANK. THEY FLEW IN WITH THIRTY-THREE HEALTHY PLANES AND THEY STAGGERED OUT WITH TWENTY-TWO OF THEM ALL CUT UP AND NOT EVEN ALL OF THOSE MADE IT BACK TO SHIPDHAM. THE KWM CLUB — JUST SOMETHING I CAME UP WITH SO I DON'T SPEND ANY LONGER THAN NECESSARY BREAKING DOWN KILLED, WOUNDED, AND MISSING IN ACTION STATISTICS — SIGNED UP FIFTY-FOUR NEW MEMBERS.

A GOOD THING THOUGH, A SILVER-LINING TYPE THING: THE PROGRAM OF LOW-LEVEL BOMBING RAIDS OVER SUBMARINE BASES IS CANCELED IMMEDIATELY. BECAUSE IT WAS SO STUPID AND CARELESS TO BEGIN WITH. NOW, ME AND THE REST OF THE CREW OF THE B-24 BATBOY ARE GOING BACK TO DOING WHAT WE DO BEST, HIGH-LEVEL BOMBING OF TRAIN DEPOTS AND VEHICLE MANUFACTUR-ING FACILITIES, MUNITIONS SITES, BALL BEARING PLANTS AND ALL THAT OTHER STUFF THE GERMANS DO SO WELL UNTIL WE STOP LETTING THEM DO IT. OH, AND BRIDGES, TOO. BRIDGE BOMBING MIGHT. BE MY FAVORITE. NOT THAT IT CHANGES MY SPECIFIC JOB ALL THAT MUCH BECAUSE WHEREVER WE GO TO DO OUR WORK, IT SEEMS A MOUNTAIN-SIZE HORNET'S NEST OPENS UP AND A WHOLE

BEVY OF THEM OLD 109S AND 190S ARE BUZZING STRAIGHT FOR ME YET AGAIN. SO MY JOB HOLDS STEADY. I SHOOT THEM, I DOWN THEM, WITH A LITTLE LUCK I KILL THEM IN ORDER TO PROTECT THE BOMBER AND THE BOMBS UNTIL THE THING BELOW THAT NEEDS TO BE DESTROYED IS DESTROYED. BUT WITH BRIDGES, THE COUNTRYSIDE IS ALMOST ALWAYS SO MUCH NICER. REMEMBER I ALWAYS LOVED BRIDGES, HANK? REMEMBER THAT? YES. YOU DON'T REMEMBER ME LOVING U-BOATS THOUGH, DO YOU?

I'M THINKING YOU HAVEN'T KILLED ANYBODY, BECAUSE THAT'S NOT YOUR JOB. BUT I'M WONDERING ABOUT THE PEOPLE AROUND YOU AND ABOUT THEM GETTING KILLED. I'M WONDERING WHAT YOU THINK AND WHAT YOU DO AND HOW YOU DO IT, AND I KNOW I WOULD DO BETTER TO HAVE YOU HERE JUST SO I COULD PICK IT UP FROM YOU. LIKE WATCHING YOUR FOOTWORK WHEN YOU WENT FOR A BALL BEHIND THE BAG AND THEN HAD TO THROW ACROSS YOUR BODY. I DON'T THINK I EVER WOULD HAVE GOT THAT MOVE DOWN ANY OTHER WAY, YOU KNOW? WHO REALLY THINKS ABOUT FOOTWORK WHEN HE THINKS ABOUT BASEBALL?

I'M OKAY THOUGH, SO DON'T YOU BE THINKING ANY-THING ELSE. JUST DON'T YOU.

We work with the Brits a lot, as you probably guessed, what with the USAAF turning about half their country into an American air base. Thing is, they have been fighting now for a LONG time. And mostly it shows. From 1939, imagine? And with the bad guys just right across that tiny little English Channel, which when I fly over it and it's one of those unusual days when we can see through the weather, I think, boy, that ain't just barely more water than the Chesapeake Bay.

I miss crab cakes something vicious.

Anyway the Brits, lots of them flying Liberators, too, so we got that whole transatlantic cousins malarkey between us all over the place, but they have been bombing their neighbors and their neighbors have been REALLY bombing, Hank, I mean PUMMELING British cities for three years already. I've been here for a couple of months and I'm ready to take my pension and go sit in a rocking chair on the porch for the rest of my life. And it's not even my country that's been getting biffed around.

They are tired, mostly, and maybe a little bit hardened beyond the point where it stops being entirely a good thing. Like, it seems reasonable that this war would be taking a toll of some kind, like on the head, right? And the Brits need to step aside for nobody else when it comes to getting in that line that pays you back compensation for all the pain and suffering you've endured. There is no such line, of course, but if there was, and there should be, well, sure, come and get it, guys, no need to be shy or shamed.

Only the boys I've seen and heard around bases and in town the few times I've gone to look around, they seem not to believe that at all. The way they talk about bomber crewmen who crack a little from too many missions flown that way and too many bombs sent this way, well it ain't nice, let me put it that way. They got a bunch of names for these guys and their afflictions like "flak happy" and "operational twitch" which are not exactly intended as compliments. I'd almost think they'd get more respect from these hardnoses if

THEY JUST DESERTED, DISAPPEARED OVER THE NEAREST HORIZON, RATHER THAN TRY AND TELL THE MILITARY WHAT'S EATING AT THEM. THEY HAVE A SPECIFIC TERM FOR GUYS WHO GET DISCHARGED FOR NERVOUS BREAKDOWN OR WHATEVER INCORRECT PSYCHOLOGICAL RESPONSE THEY DISPLAY TO YEARS AND YEARS OF SCREAMING BLUE MURDER. THE OFFICIAL RECORD SAYS "LMF," WHICH STANDS FOR "LACK OF MORAL FIBER." CAN YOU BELIEVE IT? AND THEY USE IT FOR A JOKE HERE ALL THE TIME.

IT'S A JOKE, ALL RIGHT. IT'S A JOKE, IF EVER I HEARD ONE.

AS FOR THE AIRCRAFT THEMSELVES — AND WE DO THIS WITH OURS, TOO — WHEN THEY REACH A POINT WHEN THEY CAN'T QUITE CATCH UP TO THE FASTBALL ANYMORE AND PROBABLY SHOULD BE GROUNDED FOR EVERYBODY'S SAKE, WHAT THEY DO IS THEY KEEP FLYING THEM, BECAUSE ANY ROCK IN A FIGHT, RIGHT? BUT THEY FLY THEM OFF TO THE BACK AND SIDE OF A FORMATION, THE DOGLEG, AND THEY HAVE PAINTED A BIG WW ON THEIR TAILS TO INDICATE "WAR WEARY" AIRCRAFT. SOUNDS, NOW THAT I THINK ABOUT IT, LIKE A MORE RESPECTFUL APPROACH TO THE MEN THAN THEY TAKE TO THE MACHINES.

I won't ever come down with any "operational twitch," I can assure you of that, brother. Unless they try and take away my gun, and my opportunity to shoot people. That might just give me the twitch. Otherwise, I will be right as rain. And there is an awful, awful, awful lot of rain here, so rain is right.

That would be sad, though. To come through all this only to have people thinking about you in that way. "Flak happy" they'd be whispering, or not even whispering. Sad, that would be. That would be a fearful thing to have happen, I tell you what. Puts more fear into me than the German fighter planes and they are pretty scary. But because the other stuff is scarier I am not going to tell you what I have been honestly and repeatedly thinking when I see them coming. I am not going to tell you that something inside me is convinced that those pilots, the ones I see the faces of when they are zooming close and scowling, have come for me, personally. A guy who says stuff like that is a guy who wants a big fat flak-happy stamp on his

FOREHEAD, SO IT WOULDN'T BE ME SAYING IT. IF I WAS TO SAY IT EVER THOUGH, I'D BE SAYING IT TO YOU, YOU KNOW. SO.

WW THOUGH. THAT, ON THE OTHER HAND, SOUNDS LIKE A STAMP I'D BE ALMOST PROUD TO WEAR WHEN THE TIME COMES AND I'VE EARNED IT. NOT THAT THE TIME IS LIKELY TO COME, THE WEARY TIME, BUT STILL. MAYBE I'D GET A TATTOO. TWO OF 'EM. WW AND A LIBERATOR, TOO. THE WAR WEARY LIBERATOR — NOW THAT IS A LEGACY I COULD SEE CARRYING WITH ME OUT OF THIS AWFUL TIME AND INTO THE GREAT FUTURE THIS WHOLE THING IS SUP-POSED TO BE ALL ABOUT.

AND RIGHT NOW I KNOW JUST WHAT YOU ARE DOING, HENRY McCALLUM, BECAUSE I KNOW WHAT YOU ARE LIKE. YOU ARE THINKING THAT YOUR LITTLE BROTHER HIMSELF MAY OR MAY NOT BE WAR WEARY ALREADY, BUT THAT HE IS MOST DEFINITELY LACKING MORAL FIBER.

AND AS ALWAYS, YOU ARE RIGHT. I HAVEN'T WRITTEN THEM IN FOUR MONTHS, AND THEY HAVEN'T WRIT-TEN ME. AND NO, IT DOESN'T MATTER HOW FRIGHTENING SUSAN CAN BE, AND WE ALL KNOW SHE CAN BE. THERE IS STILL NO EXCUSE FOR THIS SITUATION. I WILL

DO IT. I WILL WRITE. I WILL WRITE AND MAKE IT ALL RIGHT.

Now, YOU WRITE. I'M GOING TO WANT TO SEE THAT DIARY, AND I AM GOING TO WANT TO SEE IT FILLED. I'M MISSING ENOUGH OF OUR LIFE AS IT IS WITHOUT YOU LEAVING ANY MORE HOLES IN IT.

YOU DON'T WANT TO WIND UP BEING MICKEY ROONEY, DO YOU? NOBODY WANTS THAT. SO, PUT A LITTLE EFFORT INTO THE DIARY THING, JUST MAKE SOME EFFORT, AND I'LL SEE WHAT I CAN DO ABOUT GETTING BORIS KARLOFF FOR THE PART OF HANK. I CAN'T MAKE ANY PROMISES, BUT I'LL TALK TO SOME PEOPLE.

CHAPTER EIGHT

Best Intentions

Of course Susan is the one to write first. Of course. I had every intention of making good and writing the letter and doing my best to explain. But she is who she is, and lucky for everybody she is.

DEAR THEODORE,

FROM ME? YOU RAN AWAY, FROM ME? HOW ON EARTH ARE YOU EVER GOING TO STAND UP TO THE ENEMY IF YOUR TWELVE-YEAR-OLD SISTER SCARES YOU SO MUCH THAT YOU TURN AND RUN ALL THE WAY TO ENGLAND RATHER THAN FACE HER ONE MORE TIME?

AND THEN THERE IS THIS. YOU DON'T EVEN WRITE? WHAT IS WRONG WITH YOU? I HOPE THE REST OF OUR FORCES OVER THERE ARE BRAVER THAN YOU, BECAUSE IF THEY ARE NOT THEN WE ARE IN BIG TROUBLE. PLEASE, TELL ME YOU ARE THE BIGGEST CHICKEN WE SENT OR ELSE I AM GOING TO HAVE TO COME OVER AND fight PERSONALLY in ORDER to SAVE the family SOME dignity AND possibly the whole country.

All of which MAKES it All the STUPIDER how much I miss you AND wish you could just come home.

I miss HANK SO much SOME days I think I'm just going to fall down in the dirt AND NOT be able to get back UP AgAin. Like Pop looks All the time, AND like MAM is looking MORE AND MORE.

But HANK CAN't come home NOW, AND you CAN so MAKE SURE that you do because if SOMEHOW for SOME REASON you don't I fEAR you will be RESPON- sible for the whole family of McCAllums dying right off the MAP of AccoKEEK, MARyland, AND the world. You WANT that, THEODORE? I cERTAinly hope you do NOT.

So try AND be bRAVE. But just bRAVE ENough to fight, AND NOT bRAVE ENough to get in ANy MORE dANgER thAN NECESSARy.

And if you ARE still too chicKEN to wRite to me, you At least have to get yourself to wRite to MAM. She NEEDS that AND you KNow it.

Love,

SusAn

P.S. I know you're brave and not a chicken at all.

I have no reason to doubt that Bomber Command had the best intentions and was sincere when they announced that there would be no more low-level attacks on the submarine bases of the west coast of France.

However, while the variety of targets we attacked broadened after our first weeks in England, the truth was that U-boats were definitely not off the menu.

Nobody ever said anything about canceling high-altitude missions after all. And we flew so many of them over the fall of 1942 and the winter of 1943, that when we stop to have a look around at the beginning of March, we count fourteen B-24 Liberators left in the 44th BG.

We had started with twenty-seven only five months earlier.

But the Batboy and its crew are still intact — aside from a ding here, a dent there, and more than a few screws loose — as we stand out in the freezing rain at the Shipdham airfield, cheering like a bunch of kids at a

World Series game. We are rooting the winning run home, which in this case is badly needed reinforcements.

A whole squadron of eight new Liberators, the 506th, is winging in and touching down on the runway in front of us, along with five *extra* crews worth of replacement personnel on top of that. Meaning the new planes can take on extra shifts while our crews get some sorely needed rest time.

And as I catch up on a little rest, I run pretty well completely out of reasons not to write.

SUZIE,

OKAY, KNOCK IT OFF NOW WITH THAT THEODORE STUFF. IT'S OBVIOUS ENOUGH THAT YOU ARE MAD AT ME, AND YOU'VE GOT GOOD REASON. I OWE YOU THIS: I'M SORRY. I SHOULD NEVER HAVE RUN OFF WHEN YOU JUST WANTED A FEW MORE MINUTES WITH ME, AND YOU DESERVE WHATEVER MINUTES AND WHATEVER WORDS YOU CAN GET FROM US. EVERYTHING HAS BEEN UNFAIR, ESPECIALLY TO YOU AND MAM AND OF COURSE I WILL WRITE SOMETHING TO HER.

I JUST COULD NOT HAVE ANY MORE DISCUSSIONS WITH ANY OF YOU ABOUT HANK. HE IS MISSING, AND THAT

IS ALL. HE WILL BE BACK, HE WILL COME HOME AGAIN, I JUST KNOW IT. I HAVE FAITH, AND IF YOU GUYS DON'T HAVE ANY...WELL THAT'S JUST ABOUT THE CRAZIEST THING EVER. HOW MANY TIMES DOES THAT CHURCH OF OURS HAVE TO REMIND US TO HAVE FAITH BEFORE PEOPLE START TO PAY ATTENTION, RIGHT? ESPECIALLY SOMEBODY WITH FAITH AS STRONG AS MAM'S.

PLEASE, SUZIE, ENCOURAGE THEM. HOPE.

I JUST WISH POP HADN'T SPLIT US UP. DON'T SAY ANYTHING. BUT I GET A LITTLE ANGRY WHEN I THINK ABOUT IT, THAT HANK AND I WOULD STILL BE TOGETHER, FIGHTING SIDE BY SIDE LIKE ALWAYS, IF HE HADN'T GONE AND MADE US SEPARATE LIKE HE DID.

LOVE, THEO (WITHOUT THE DORE)

It's the biggest operation yet for the Flying Eight-Balls of the 44th as we approach yet another submarine base. This time, though, it's in Germany itself, and it is a massive operation as over two hundred aircraft of the Eighth Air Force hit four German targets at once. Around two-thirds of those, including us, go for the base at Kiel.

The B-17s all fly in formation ahead of us and so we know well ahead of time that we are heading into the most intense resistance we have ever seen. The explosions in the air and on the ground are earsplitting long before the formation of B-24s reaches the target area. Gallagher is at the right cheek gun and Bell at the left as we all anticipate the ferocious fight to come.

The sky is black with flak and buzzing with fighters as we see the Fortresses absorb the first wave of the attack. Before we can make out who is where in the fight ahead we know the unmistakable flash and ping of direct hits on aircraft and the popcorn popping of Messerschmitts and Focke-Wulf fighters exchanging fire with our bombers at close range and every angle.

The German planes come straight out of the blackness like swooping, shrieking nightmares as we enter the IP and our bombardier dives into his position on the floor. I have that little bit more elbow room as my gun judders away like it's going to dislocate both my elbows. Bell stays in position on my left, firing away just as heavily into the growing flock of fighters coming straight at us.

It is not personal, as I have learned over the months. I had thought maybe it was me they had it in for, but it's only that both the B-17 and the B-24 are most vulnerable to frontal attacks, which avoid the bulk of our heavy artillery spread around the body of the aircraft. Somehow that knowledge is little relief, as we are peppered with heavy shells whistling past and punching holes in the plane just the same.

We give as good as we get, though, as Bell and I have gotten very familiar with the nose-to-nose fighting. Nobody gets past us. One after another of their aircraft takes a pounding as it passes the nose cone, trailing smoke before even being greeted by Couley's top turret guns, then Quinn and Dodge pounding from the waist, and Boyd sitting in wait at the tail.

Gallagher is screaming something about the target and Ormston and Lowrie are snapping back and forth up on the pilots' deck, and none of it means anything to us up front because we can't see anything that isn't right in front of us until it either explodes in the sky or swoops in to attack us point blank.

Gallagher screams louder as he takes over and the bombing begins ahead of us.

The most massive coordinated release of tonnage I've seen is dropped by one after another after another Flying Fortress, and it is everything I ever thought the end of the world would sound like. Flak is still dogging all of us but there is some clearing of sight lines after the drops are made.

Because the sky ahead is rapidly clearing of traffic.

Fighters and bombers alike are bursting into flame, billowing smoke, breaking completely apart like I have never seen before. It feels as if the entire air war is being decided here, today, right now, as the bombs begin thudding into targets below, and planes crash spectacularly, and the huge formation of B-17s that remains flying take their formation as one great flock and bank away out of the target zone.

Leaving our much smaller formation of B-24s to finish the job.

A whole new wave of fighters comes up to take us on as the flak continues to batter our guys. We no longer have the protection of the lead planes and their guns, nor the strength of numbers, as we are now one quarter of the force that set out this morning.

There is a massive blast that I can see out of the

corner of my eye, one Liberator torn basically to shreds by both flak and fighter fire at once. It makes a bigger noise than the bombs as it shoots toward the earth.

Gallagher is going crazy now, screaming something nobody on earth but himself could ever understand except that we all know what it means.

The telltale whistling of our own bombs begins as the bomb bay doors open and we drop our load of extra special ordnance on the submarine base of Kiel.

We are taking heavy hits now, but we knew we would and we know why we have to.

The Fortresses dropped a heavy load of high explosives, and we are following with incendiaries that work together with those bombs to basically double the explosiveness of everything, as if we sent a whole second mission in on top of this one. We are paying the price, as one Liberator after another is hit, our formation small and exposed to such a big resistance force. But we also feel the success of it all as the whole world beneath us feels like it explodes, then explodes, then explodes again. The heat of the fire coming up from under our belly is intense, insane, and pushes us off like a smoky surf as the remaining bombers bank in formation and get out of here finally, swooping away home.

There is a feeling of great satisfaction as we tuck into a tight grouping for the long limp back to base. It was also a lot lonelier as barely more than a dozen of us are flying back, between the losses we've suffered and the Fortresses having already broken off. Several of the planes are trailing smoke, some with at least one engine failing to function.

Nobody talks, as we all concentrate on just nursing the aircraft back.

Mam,

I know it has been too long. I'm sorry. It was a lot of things, but most of all, it has been crazy busy here in the air over Europe.

But the good news is that your boy gets to write to you now as a certified hero. That's because there is a certificate to prove it. Our group, the 44th Bombers, received the DUC — Distinguished Unit Citation — for doing a pretty good job of messing up some German U-boat operations that

HAVE BEEN CAUSING BIG PROBLEMS THE WHOLE WAR. IT WASN'T THAT DANGEROUS OR ANYTHING, SO CALM DOWN, BUT WE HAVE GOTTEN SO GOOD AT WHAT WE DO THAT WE EXCEEDED EVERYBODY'S EXPECTATIONS (ESPECIALLY THE GERMANS!), AND REALLY DID A JOB ON THEM.

WE ARE THE FIRST UNIT OF THE EIGHTH AIR FORCE TO RECEIVE A DUC!

SO YOU SEE ALL IS GOING AS WELL AS IT COULD BE OVER HERE. IF WE KEEP IT UP AT THIS RATE I AM SURE WE WILL BE ABLE TO FINISH THESE GUYS OFF SOON, AND THEN I WILL BE HOME TO SEE YOU AGAIN IN NO TIME.

SAY HI TO POP, AND LOVE TO SUSAN, AND DON'T WORRY AND KEEP FAITH AND HOPE, RIGHT? SAY A COUPLE EXTRA PRAYERS, AND SEE WHAT THAT GETS US.

MEANWHILE I HAVE TO GET BACK TO ALL THAT WAR-WINNING STUFF NOW.

I WILL WRITE AGAIN SOON, I PROMISE.

LOVE,

THEO

CHAPTER NINE

On the Fly

So, are you writing, ya big goon? Because I'm writing, to the girls. 'Cause YOU made me feel guilty about it. So your diary had better be filling up so that when we get together you have at least a little something to contribute to the exchange.

Not that you stand much of a chance of keeping up with my stuff anyway.

I have a Distinguished Unit Citation. Well, not just me. I had some help, so they gave it to the whole 44th Bomber Group. It's a pretty big deal in the Air Corps. The DUC.

Truth is, brother, we earned it.

A whole skyload of B-17s dumped about a zillion high explosives on a sub base and then hightailed it while a relatively small bunch of us B-24s followed them in with a drop of incendiaries. Which is basically like one group starting the

FIRE AND THE NEXT GROUP BLOWING THE GASOLINE AND FLAMING TORCHES ALL OVER IT. WE PRETTY NEAR ROASTED OURSELVES OVER OUR OWN BARBECUE, IS THE TRUTH OF THE MATTER. BUT WE DEVASTATED A WHOLE LOT OF LUFTWAFFE AIRCRAFT AS WELL AS THOSE NASTY, SNEAKY U-BOATS.

WE ALSO LEARNED WHAT OUR ENGINEER WAS TALKING ABOUT WITH THE LIBERATOR'S FLAWS. EVERYBODY WAS HURTING, HANK, MANY PLANES AND MANY MEN LEFT BEHIND ON THAT RAID. AND THE RAGGEDY RUMP OF THE MISSION THAT WAS US, THE LAST DOZEN OR SO B-24S, WERE ALL IN ONE STATE OR ANOTHER OF INJURED.

BUT WE KNEW THE CREW LANDING JUST IN FRONT OF US WAS IN DESPERATE SHAPE. THESE DAVIS WINGS THAT RIDE SO HIGH ON THE FUSELAGE MAKE FOR FAST FLYING AND TRICKY LANDING IF THINGS AIN'T RIGHT. AND GAS TANKS, THEY SNAKE EVERYWHERE TO SAVE SPACE, EVEN INTO THE WINGS.

SO THE BOAT IN FRONT OF US, WE CAN SEE IT WEAVING AND WOBBLING, TRYING TO LAND LEVEL WITH THREE ENGINES RUNNING, TWO OF THEM BILLOWING SMOKE, THE TAIL COMING IN HIGHER THAN NORMAL UNTIL BAM, THEY HIT FOR A BELLY LANDING HARD ENOUGH WE

CAN FEEL IT OURSELVES, AND THOSE WINGS JUST FOLD, COLLAPSE ON IMPACT, RIGHT DOWN OVER THE BODY OF THE PLANE AND ONTO THE GROUND LIKE SOME GREAT EAGLE BIRD THAT HAS JUST QUIT ON ITSELF, DROPPED WINGS, AND SKIDDED AWAY TO DIE. WHICH IS WHAT IT DID BASICALLY, HANK. ONLY EAGLES DON'T BURST INTO FLAMES WHEN THEY CRASH, AS FAR AS I KNOW.

WE COULD NOT BELIEVE WHAT WE WERE SEEING, EVEN THOUGH EVERYBODY IN THE WHOLE EIGHTH HAS HEARD ABOUT THIS BEFORE. AND THE FLAME WAS SO BIG, SO QUICK AND HOT, THAT WE HAD TO EVEN ABORT OUR LANDING, PILOT AND COPILOT SHOUTING OVER THE INTERCOM AS WE PULLED RIGHT UP, FEELING THAT BIG FLAME JUST LIKE WE FELT IT UNDER OUR BELLIES ON THE MISSION. ONLY THIS TIME WE ALL STRAINED, LOOKING THROUGH ALL THE GLASS WINDOWS AND BUBBLES AS WE PULLED UP AND FLEW OVALS OVER OUR PARTNER CRAFT AND CREW AS IT SPUN FIERY CIRCLES AND FINALLY CAME TO STOP, AND EVERY LAST GROUND CREWMAN SCRAMBLED TO DO SOMETHING 'CAUSE THOSE GUYS ARE GREAT, THEY REALLY ARE, BUT WE KNEW EVEN FROM ALTITUDE THAT THERE WAS NOTHING. NOTHING.

SO THAT IS ONE FLAW CONFIRMED, ABOUT THIS GREAT AIRCRAFT.

AND IT'S NOT EXACTLY THE VERSION I PASSED ALONG
TO MAM, JUST SO YOU KNOW.

AND IT'S ONE MORE REASON I DON'T EXPECT YOUR
DIARY TO TOP MY DIARY, MISTER.

AND ONE MORE REASON I SURE HOPE IT DOESN'T.

We're leaving England for a little while very shortly. We are off missions and on special training to learn a few new tricks before we get loaned out to the Ninth Air Force. Seems like we are getting noticed, because we're so popular that three bomber groups of Liberators have been requested for temporary duty, flying out of North Africa.

I wonder if I'll miss the rain? Pretty sure I won't.

One day in early June, however, I wake up to a morning so sunny and warm I sit up in bed for several minutes, disoriented, trying my hardest to work out if I'm dreaming, or if maybe I have gotten so deep into this life which isn't a life that I have entirely forgotten that we have already decamped to Libya.

Then, the kid who brings the mail around comes to me with a letter.

"Mornin', Sergeant," he says as he hands it to me. "Beautiful day, ain't it? Better get outside while you can, knowing how lazy the English sun is."

"Thanks, I will," I say and tear the letter open.

Son,

Your father and I could not be prouder of you. Your citation is something we can scarcely imagine, what bravery and danger must have been involved. Pop in particular is well aware that they do not throw these things around like paper airplanes (his words, of course), and that your group must have done extraordinary things to have earned it. So do not go thinking that anyone here is buying your rather casual account of events in your letter. We do appreciate, however, your kindness in trying not to over worry us. We hope that someday you will feel relaxed enough about it all to give us a fuller accounting. But as I am still waiting for such accountings from your father regarding his experience in the last one of these terrible things, I have much patience prepared for you.

The Navy has been good to their word, writing every three months to keep us current on your brother's official status. It is a formality, of course, but it is also a courtesy and one we do appreciate. To know that Henry's service and sacrifice are not disregarded so easily is a comfort to us, albeit a small one.

His name has still not appeared on any of the other lists they revise constantly, so he remains as of today, missing in action. By the time you get this it will have been officially one year.

I would write more if I could, Theodore, but I cannot. But I will do so very soon. Everyone is thinking of you, and proud of you, and anxious to see you again.

Love,

Mam and Pop

I check the calendar. June 6, 1943.

Happy anniversary, brother. Where should I send your card?

We spend several weeks doing something we were never trained to do back in the United States, flying once again in much lower formations than we are supposed to. But it's not like the time we spent going low over the subs, striking fear into the hearts of Nazis and tuna alike. Instead we spend our days terrorizing small villages all over the British countryside as we practice running raids over land at treetop level.

What we find out is that we are a far more experienced and skilled bomber group than the one that first attempted formation flying at low levels. And that our trusty and tough, scarred but reliable B-24 can do whatever we need it to do, as long as *we* are up to the job.

Just as I'm getting used to a view of British trees and little else, we receive orders to ship out to our new temporary home: the base at Benghazi, Libya. The Allies have finally finished the task of pushing the Germans and Italians all the way off of North Africa, which raises the question of what our task will be. But it is a question that does not weigh too heavily on us. As we fly over the Mediterranean, everyone is noticeably more upbeat and confident than we have been for some time. Despite all the secrecy, there is a feeling that we know what's coming. Or, rather that we know what we're coming for. And we cannot wait to get started.

"It's the invasion," Boyd says as I settle down into his tail turret. One of the things we've had the time to do, between all the training and the long-haul flight, is get all the gunners more familiar with one another's stations. Just in case.

"Invasion of what?" I say, a little distracted by how much I am enjoying the turret. Its maneuverability, its practicality. Everything seems handy, natural, well planned, and *modern* compared to the greenhouse up front.

"Italy, McCallum. The beginning of the end. Haven't you been paying attention? Churchill called it the 'soft underbelly' of Nazi Europe, and I think he's right."

"I want one of these," I say, still remaining on my own personal turret mission, flattening the enemy regardless of where we invade.

"I don't really see what makes it any softer than the rest of Nazi Europe," Dodge says from his radioman perch. "I mean, it is still crammed with, you know, Italians and Germans."

"I can't wait to invade Italy," Hargreaves says from the top turret where Couley normally shoots from. "Everybody says the Italians aren't nearly as hard to handle as the Germans."

"I'm inclined to agree with you," Couley says, from Hargreaves's belly gun position.

"How come you're agreein' with him?" Quinn says. He has just emerged into the tail area, calling back in Couley's direction. "You ain't never once agreed with me, I don't think."

"Sure he has," Boyd says loud enough for everybody's entertainment. "Couley thinks you're nutty, and you *know* you are."

It is definitely a lighter-hearted group, a more easygoing journey, than any I can remember.

Quinn actually goes to the trouble of physically waving down the laughter coming from the direction of each crewman, like we've all released a stink in his direction at the same time. Then he points hard at me. "You, McCallum, how is it that you ain't lookin' like an orange left out in the sun all summer?"

I look at him for a few seconds, hoping to get a better read on him, then turn to Boyd. "You usually understand what he says, right? Translate for me."

"Quinn," Boyd barks while simultaneously motioning me out of his seat. "What are you talking about, kid?"

"I'm talking about that glass nursery where this guy spends all his time. I was only there for a half hour and my head felt like an August tomato that was about to burst out of its skin. I guess that explains all the red splatter we usually see all over the front of these things, huh?"

"Well, all right," I say, jumping up and scooting happily to my home station. "Boys, it sounds like we are closing in on our sunny new home base."

"Don't get used to it," Lieutenant Ormston orders as I pass the pilot's perch. "Temporary. This is just a detachment for a short period."

No offense to England, but I might have trouble detaching from real sunshine again, even after only a short period.

We are only a few weeks into our North Africa journey when I am proven wrong about the constantly sunny and pleasant conditions I expected we would be enjoying. But at the same time, and more important and as usual, Sergeant Boyd is proven right, as we fly through rough rainy weather at the forefront of the Allied invasion of the island of Sicily.

We pass over a huge flotilla of American and British ships carrying armored and infantry divisions that look like they would have the strength to take the whole continent, let alone an island.

Still, we've been asked to clear the way, and we are an accomodating crew. We pass over the southern coast of Sicily and almost immediately reach the IP, and Gallagher takes his spot at the sights and prepares to take over the controls.

"Milk run!" Bell yells from behind me, working his navigation table as there is no need for him at the gun.

Guys start yelling it out all over the craft. "Milk run" you can hear through the intercom and all around us until the pilot commands everybody to shut up and mind their jobs.

Milk run is the term guys use for a mission so easy you might as well be delivering the morning milk around your hometown for all the danger you are in. Some guys don't like to use the term ever, feeling like that's just overconfidence and a kind of *asking for it* that a war situation really doesn't need.

It's one of the rare opinions I share with Lieutenant Ormston.

Dodge is at his radioman duties, Couley doing whatever it is an engineer does when everything on the ship seems to be doing what it's supposed to be doing. Even the guys who are manning their guns, like me, are rigid with readiness but not any more occupied than that. There is simply no fighter resistance coming up to greet us.

Gallagher announces that he is within a minute or so from being over target, which is only going to make resistance less likely. We are in one of a number of USAAF and RAF formations that are strictly here softening the ground for the real job of taking total and swift control of the island. As Gallagher whoops and releases our singsong explosives down toward the airfield below, we seem to have caught them entirely by surprise.

The weather remains nasty, and we are almost as freezing cold as we were when we flew missions out of Shipdham. We are all taking our oxygen through masks as we bomb from nearly twenty-five thousand feet, where we feel the first ineffectual bursts of antiaircraft rockets only seconds before the explosions start pop-pop-pop-popping their planes and facilities down below into the mud.

It is eerily flat up here as we finish unloading and the whole formation starts banking for home. There is something like silence, the lack of resistance a nice change from the fury we have faced on so many other missions. But it is, of course, a relative silence as the engines all around us roar as big as they ever have.

At one point, three or four minutes after we have locked onto our homeward trajectory and begin to make visual contact with what the air and sea forces are bringing to the enemy, Dodge breaks our internal quiet with a short "Everybody awake?" over the radio. He gets a few comical answers, one snore, one shut up, and at least one total silence from the team members.

From my perch at the tip of the glass I can more clearly see the forces coming in stages from the other direction. We descend some, breaking through lower and lighter clouds in time to see a wave of British fighters, Hurricanes and Hellcats, scorch past beneath us. They are leading a barrage of another element I have only heard about before now. Well over one hundred RAF gliders, engineless troop transports, are being towed by American C-47 Dakotas. The gliders are bigger than I thought they would be and don't look all that comfortable in the current swirly conditions. They wobble a lot in the trail of the sturdy old Dakotas, and I must say, with their high wings and plump midsection, I'm glad there are no B-17 guys around to point out the visual similarity between the gliders and the Liberator.

The air attack is long behind us and the massive ground attack already hitting the beaches as we reach the relative calm of our runway at Benghazi. It feels as close as we have come to a routine day at the office on this job, and all I can say is I hope our time here is filled with nothing but milk runs like this.

"You can take your mask off now, Sergeant Couley, *Life Magazine* ain't here today," I hear the copilot, Lowrie, say as the engines cut out and guys prepare to hand the plane over to the ground crew for routine maintenance. I don't usually hear Lowrie say much at all to the lower ranks of our crew, and every time he does I'm reminded why I'm glad I don't.

"Couley! Couley, man, wake up!" It's Dodge yelling and the unfamiliar squeal in his voice makes it clear this is no fooling. The guys from the nose start climbing over each other to get through the narrow space leading back to the midsection. We can hear already more urgency than we've heard all day as we tumble through and find Dodge and Hargreaves dragging

Couley to the floor and tearing his suit open, his mask away.

They are trying to revive him, blowing into him, shoving down on him. Boyd scrambles back toward the rear exit and jumps out. Quinn jumps in when Dodge throws himself back at the radio and starts shouting into it for the medics to get to us.

Two medics are there in seconds, scurrying up the route Boyd just took the other way. They shove their way through and brush our guys back as they try and try to get something like breath coming in and out of our guy, our engineer.

We all stand rigid as the medics stop all that and frantically pull Couley toward the rear opening, where a team of other medical staff are bellowing for them to do that and get him out before it's too late.

They are good, those boys, and they give it everything, and they look so distressed you have to believe they care, no matter how many times they have run through this same bleak routine.

But everybody who sees the Couley we see, gray-blue and floppy as they drag him away, knows that *too late* has already come and gone.

I look away, waiting for the rescue team to clear the area before I make any move at all. I see when I do that the officers are going over everything up at the engineer's position, in the bubble beneath his top gunner turret.

Lieutenant Ormston has the hose in his hand, the one that connects Couley's mask to the oxygen supply. He's pulling at it, hard, and looking up to Lowrie as they both nod, seeing the tube pinched tight, caught in the gear of the gunner's swiveling turret mechanism.

One thing everybody knows around here without needing to be told is that we move on. No matter what, we just move on.

Couley was so determined to be right about everything that he died showing us one of the sneakiest hazards of working on the B-24, with its high-altitude capacity, lack of cabin pressure, and imperfect oxygen supply system. He was a good guy and a good teammate and he was on the ball regarding the things he warned us about. Now he's gone and we move on with a new engineer/top turret gunner.

He is named Hollings and is available to us as the result of being the only survivor of a Liberator crew that had to ditch in the desert of Tunisia in the very last days of the North Africa Campaign. A tank company found him walking in the direction of his base a couple days later.

Seems like a nice enough guy, Hollings, and smart as Couley was, but he also has eyes that look to have seen enough already and that point in slightly different directions so I don't see us buddying up all that much.

So, we move on. Batboy moves on without Sergeant Couley just as the invasion of Sicily moves on largely without any more need for the Batboy. In the weeks following our attack on that airfield kicking off Operation Husky, General Patton's tanks take the beach and grind their way up one side of the island while Field Marshal Montgomery's British armored divisions push up the other and we are removed from the plan altogether.

I briefly consider that maybe even Boyd could guess wrong as we spend all of our time once again practicing seriously low-level bombing raids against inland targets. All the practice eventually reaches dress-rehearsal stage when five full bomber groups carry out a mock raid on a huge dummy installation that had been built in the desert just for us.

Finally, August arrives, and we know.

The same five groups, nearly two hundred B-24s, leave the ground through heavy weather once again, and from early on, this feels like something different. We are the fourth of the five and receive constant reports of what the lead groups are encountering. An hour into the flight there is a lot of radio commotion, a lot of chatter among radioman, pilot, copilot, and navigator. Eventually we are notified that ten aircraft have had difficulties and had to abort out of the lead group.

Two hours later there is a similar ruckus as Dodge frantically relays the transmission coming from the front of the formation. The lead plane on the lead group is having severe trouble.

"He's wavering all over!" Dodge calls out. "Now he's upright, climbing, not climbing . . . oh, my, he's down, the lead navigator craft is on its back in the water, going down. Second lead circles back for rescue . . . holy cow, two lead planes of the entire mission are out! Number three plane now leads."

It is hard for me to even fathom that kind of importance at the front of such a huge mission. The Batboy is middle of the pack, second from last grouping, and even our nose gunner is right now sweating right through his sheepskin at the pressure here. We are flying so low, we can see the shadow of every aircraft on the water below us. The formation holds as far as I can tell, but as far as I can tell is only as far as I can see our wingmen and that's not telling much of the big picture. That picture is coming slightly more into focus as the radio exchanges tell of increasing separation of the first two groups. Our officers sound something less than their usual confident selves.

We are carrying huge and uncommon firepower, both five-hundred- and one-thousand-pound demolition bombs, as well as incendiaries. Ground crew engineers somehow found space to fit extra fuel tanks inside the bomb-bay compartment, and we find out the importance of that when it takes us nearly five hours to even approach the destination.

The weather has been awful the whole way, and I confess I am a little nervous when, for the first time ever, Lieutenant Ormston has left his pilot's position and is right behind me conferring with Bell over the navigator's table. We were supposed to take a route over the mountains of Yugoslavia and Albania, but the conditions were so heavy that we have had to take an even longer route around them. Their words make it clear we are now approaching the border of Bulgaria, and my nerves jangle all the harder when I feel the reality of it hit. We really are going for it. We're going to attack Ploesti, the gigantic oil installation that is said to fuel a huge percentage of enemy operations across the European Theater.

This has been tried before, with little luck. But when we sent a mission over before, it wasn't one tenth the size of this force so everybody knows this is on a scale of difficulty and importance that probably adds up to all our other missions combined.

It seems to be bearing that out as we come within range of the mission destination. The first two groups are way farther ahead than they were supposed to be so it becomes almost like two separate, smaller strike forces sixty miles apart. Way off of a plan that would need to heed every detail to have a chance.

Ploesti's a giant collection of oil-processing installations that ring around a medium-size city, and each of our groups has an assigned target within the general zone. The final group, just behind us, breaks off to the north as we approach the first IP, the town of Pitesti. The plan from here is for each of the other groups to proceed counterclockwise around the IP perimeter, then peel off at the designated point to attack its individual target.

As soon as we have left the first group to their assignment, the rest of us drop down to a level of just five hundred feet. Couley could have breathed freely here.

We are in essence a two BG attack now as the two lead groups are someplace far off, hopefully in the direction of their assignment. We have retained contact with our partners in the group just ahead, and the plan is for us to remain locked together for the duration of the mission.

Ormston, up in the boss's chair, hollers in through the intercom for Bell to update him and Bell is quick to let him know we have identified our target, the town of Floresti, and we're on a course straight for it.

I am glued to my machine gun, with Gallagher right up against me at the right cheek gun. But he keeps leaning in the direction of his bombardier sights, itching to jump on the task he came for.

Off in the distance, in several distances it seems, we

hear the old familiar sounds of an enemy defending itself from a bomber attack. There is far-off fury that already sounds like a new order of mayhem from what we have known before, and it's all fingers crossed from here in the hope that every group does its job, and we join up real soon for a relatively healthy formation home.

But before we even get close enough for Gallagher to take the controls, the defenses are all over us, attacking from all sides and in numbers that make it plain we have come as no surprise to anybody.

"What is this?" Bell screams as he abandons navigating for some much more important machine gunning. He and I are battering straight ahead at both German and Romanian fighters who are slinging a variety of heavy artillery our way.

I have no answer for him other than just hollering wordless sound behind my firing, to buck myself up more than anything else.

Flak is with us as usual, but there are distinctly larger shells going off among them. One explodes just below us somewhere around the tail and our B-24 almost flips a somersault with the impact beneath us.

Two seconds later we dip to an angle perpendicular to the ground as one of those shells slams into our left wingman, decimating the plane, scattering metal and Liberator crew body parts in every direction, including a shower of the whole mess spraying across my glass.

It is every bit the fight of our lives as we right ourselves and bear in on our target refineries dead ahead.

One of them is smoking heavily from a bombing that has already happened, and I realize we are flying into a burning furnace, far lower than any bomber should.

Gallagher starts his best shouting that is beginning to be among my favorite sounds, and the pilots cease their so far incredible maneuvering among fighter rounds and antiaircraft shells, through blinding smoke and plummeting dead aircraft, and for a few seconds every man on board becomes meaningless to our supreme bombardier's inexplicable magic pathfinding straight to the big, ugly refinery that is ours.

Booo-hooooo-hooooo-hoooom! go the explosions as the refinery erupts like a squat volcano. We witness the first couple of booms ourselves, as they go off before our bombs land. It's the delayed explosion of some of our partner group's payload. The fire and pressure of the combination shoots us straight up as we pass over the refinery on a column of smoke and fire that could eventually reach other planets.

The lead plane of our group is still visible as we waffle out of the chaos that is the target sight. We follow closely as a web of B-24s from the rear end of the giant raid hangs together as tightly as we dare, but as deftly as we had learned in the countryside of England and over the desert of Libya.

The remainders of us, the two groups who had been pointed at the town of Floresti since starting our engines in Benghazi this morning, cling to the last bits of mission plan together. With flak still very large and real all around us, we follow the final directions closely, banking right, hanging tight, heading back to North Africa.

But it turns out, naturally, not to be anywhere near that easy. We are chased, through the inferno that is Ploesti, across the IP, and on into Albania, where Bulgarian fighters converge on a Liberator that is struggling to keep up, with trouble in three engines. It is sickening to listen as they shred the straggler with enough firepower to down it ten times over, following the plane and crew almost all the way to the massive crash to the ground.

It is not until we are out a substantial distance over open water that we are finally rid of the pursuit. Even though I feel my body relax enough to take my hands off the gun handles for the first time since I last saw this sea, I feel in shock. The barely noticeable sounds and movements of a crew still doing all the necessary jobs as best they can, attest to the shared feelings all around.

But our pilot steps up into the moment to acknowledge the other part, over the speaker. "Gentlemen, that mess was the best thing you ever made."

It was. It was the best, and it was a mess, and we did our job.

There is still only ocean on the horizon when Ormston calls out to Hollings "What do you figure?" he says, asking a question that only they have apparently considered.

"Can't see us making it, frankly, sir."

The fuel situation has reached critical, as it surely has for the handful of other planes trying to make it back to Africa alongside us, and the ones farther flung with the same aim.

Dodge is busy on the radio, searching for possible

solutions, any dry land we might reach. There is controlled excitement when he and the pilots and Bell end a frantic round of conversation with an agreed plan, a mini-formation banking sharply to the left, and deep sighs of breath all over for the next half hour.

The joy of the glass nose cone is being first to see whatever we have coming, as it appears, then teases, then seems to move away as the plane begins the cough and splutter. Then it becomes real, becomes the truth and becomes possible without ever becoming less miraculous.

"Hold on, strap in, prepare for impact," Ormston calls out as we all holler out and hunker down just before the bump of the tall tree punches our belly, then we hit solid earth with a bang, then another bang, then a crunch. We skid across the field, the intended airstrip still in sight a quarter mile ahead. The Liberator does its thing and folds up its wings, the roof feeling like it's caving in on us, but it doesn't, and we bang a few times more, roll, rock, and shock until skidding to a stop on the most delicious dollop of island in the world.

Buongiorno, Sicily.

*   *   *

I am not even aware of how much of an impact I've absorbed on the landing because I am so ecstatic to have landed at all.

Hollings turns out to be just as good a guy as the last engineer. He quickly wends his way through the crunch to check on the three of us who are all packed into the very front edge of the plane together, like pork stuffed into a sausage casing. "Are you hurt?" he says nervously, easing us out of our lump and into sitting position on the remaining square of floor in front of the navigator's table.

"I think I'm okay," I say. Sitting, cautiously running my hands over my bones to take inventory.

"Tell me something," Gallagher says, brushing Hollings off and making his way past, "do your planes *ever* make it all the way home?"

Bell stares uncomprehendingly, blood streaming from a gash at his hairline. "Who's this?" he asks me, pointing at Hollings.

I smile, point at him, and notice my own hand covered in blood. I reach back up to my head to check for the source, but don't recall finding it.

*　　*　　*

The possibilities are that I'm dead, still unconscious, or a very old man recalling things in no particular order when I hear a sharp and grating Boston accent asking me if I'm the same jerk who always used to slide into second with his spikes up.

I open my eyes. I'm on a stretcher, on the ground, next to Bell, who is in the same situation only unconscious. Not far off to my right is the collapsed hulk of the remarkable B-24 Batboy with both US Army and Air Corps personnel climbing over and through the corpse of the great ship roughly, like it was just a plane.

Looming over me to my left is a vehicle that looks like the back half of a tank welded onto the front half of a cargo truck, with a machine gun mounted on the roof. Crouching low between the mutant vehicle and me is another curious beast in camouflage.

"Oh, no," I say, though each word bangs another nail into my sore skull. "Can it be? Can you really be that gimpy Red Sox meathead first baseman?"

"I am that very meathead," he says with a wide grin. "Roman Bucyk." He sticks out a hand and gives me a warm grip. He shakes, and does so gently, which must take some restraint for him.

"So," I say, "did I die and go to the Eastern Shore league for my sins?"

"Yup," he says, "stuck on the Federalsburg A's for all eternity."

A second soldier hops down from the back of the half-track and comes to take one end of Bell's stretcher. Bucyk slides over to take the other end and the two of them load him into the back of the truck. Then they ferry a few more soldiers to the truck, and finally Bucyk and his partner gather me up.

"Where am I going?" I ask as they bump along and slide me in last.

"Field hospital, couple miles," he says.

I am suddenly and surprisingly kind of desperate for a little more of the meathead's time. I reach out and grab his wrist.

"I'll see you there. I'm the guy driving you," he says with a wicked grin that fills me with both reassurance and alarm.

My head is stitched up by the time he comes around to see me. They have checked me out and so far nothing alarming is showing up, though there is no part of me that isn't in pain inside and out. I don't know where the rest of the crew has been taken, but medics assure me every time they come by that everybody is being taken good care of.

"You look not so bad," Bucyk says, standing beside my bed. "Seen ya look worse."

"Thanks," I say. Between the pain, the lingering shock of the crash, the mission, the war, and everything else, it's all kinds of strange enough without trying to have a conversation with this character just now. Even stranger is the fact that I want to.

I'm not sure where to start, but after several lingering seconds of nothing, he jumps in. "I'm really sorry about your brother," he says in a new gravelly tone.

"So, you heard about it," I say, looking down.

"Yeah," he says. "My girl . . . you might remember Hannah, played for Centreville Ladies, better arm than any of us? Anyway, she's from right around there and so, she stays informed, local news and all that. The paper there has been very respectful, locals and Shore League boys alike. They post it all, and she sends it to me. Just so I can see how the home front feels about the guys doing it overseas. Nice."

I hear the rustling of paper and look up to see him taking a well-folded copy of a familiar eight-page weekly from his breast pocket.

I take it from him and start reading the part I am obviously meant to read. It is indeed respectful, a nicely set roll call of local sacrifice to the effort.

"Bill Thomas," he says when I don't respond immediately. "You remember Bill Thomas. Teammate of mine in Centreville. Hit .270. Air Corps pilot, went down right near where I was at during Operation Torch. Losing teammates all over, seems. I'm really sorry, Theo."

He is awkward, and stumbling, but he sure is giving it a go. It is jarring to hear him say my name, just as I reach my brother's spot on the list.

Where it says KILLED IN ACTION.

"It's a typo," I say, folding it up calmly and handing it back to him. "He's still listed MIA. They haven't found him yet, is all. Dumb ol' local papers anyway, huh?"

"Yeah," he says, jamming the dumb ol' paper roughly back in that pocket behind his Bucyk name tag.

"They might send you home now," he says, pointing oddly at various parts of me to apparently identify injuries.

"I don't think it's that bad," I say.

"Well," he says, and with his offer of another shake he signals the end of our visit, "make sure you get back somehow, eventually. Get yourself back to baseball. I know I reached my limit and, while I never cared much for you guys, y'know, you could play. Both of you were real ballplayers." Our handshake is finished now, and he is backing away from it. "You could, you should play again. Get home and do it."

He is just about gone when I call him back with a "hey," and he turns. "Nazis *hate* baseball," I say, shaking a fist.

"Don't they ever," he says, shaking his fist in return.

CHAPTER TEN

Keeping Score

We lost fifty-four Liberators and over five hundred airmen in the Operation Tidal Wave raid on Ploesti. And despite so much of it not going at all to plan, we still wound up giving the oil operations a pretty good mauling that they will feel for a good long time. There's real job satisfaction in knowing your work is noted and remembered.

The USAAF noted us with our second DUC and each man also earned the Distinguished Flying Cross.

I am surprised to find the return to Shipdham at the end of August feels a little like a homecoming. The whole crew has made it back, and our aircraft is a shiny new B-24J. I have a turret finally, where the glass-house was on Batboy, and that alone is an exciting development. There is also a retractable belly turret for Hargreaves, where the old plane just had that gun poking straight through the floor.

In addition to a new plane, mail is waiting for me on my return.

DEAR BROTHER,

So, it sounds like you ARE going to win this thing all by yourself now. OR at least you and your little gang. MAM and POP want me to tell you how bursting their buttons they ARE with PRIDE (because they surely ARE not getting fat these days) over all the awards and citations and medals and commendations and whatnot you ARE collecting. ARE you going to look like a general or something with all your decorations when you come home? You have been in the PAPER, which maybe you did not know so I am including it here. You ARE now an official hero instead of just the kind you were before.

MAM is not quite up to writing so you will just have to do with me, so I hope that's okay. EVERYbody sends love though. EVERYBODY.

And, THEO, I meant to try and write you sooner. I did, but I need to tell you, we heard again from the NAVY, about HANK, and it was a *lot sooner than three months this time because they had something —*

We are just about settled back into England and warmed up to our new aircraft when word comes that we are being detached again to North Africa.

ARE YOU WRITING? ARE YOU KEEPING UP, AND KEEPING SCORE? IT PROBABLY ISN'T EVEN WORTH THE EFFORT ANYMORE BECAUSE YOU COULD FIGHT TEN MORE OF THESE WARS JUST AS BIG AS THIS ONE AND STILL NOT KEEP UP WITH ME.

STILL, YOU SHOULD KEEP AT IT. BECAUSE I WILL WANT TO KNOW. WHEN WE GET BACK TOGETHER AND YOU AND I COMPARE ADVENTURES, I WILL STILL WANT TO KNOW. BECAUSE WHATEVER THE DIFFERENCE, YOU ARE IMPORTANT TO ME. WHATEVER YOU DO IS STILL IMPORTANT TO ME EVEN IF WHATALL I DO IS SO MUCH MORE AND BIGGER AND I HAVE NO MORE CHEST SPACE FOR THE AWARDS THEY WANT TO PIN ON ME. BUT I FIGURE, I WOULDN'T HAVE HALF THE CHEST I HAVE IF IT WASN'T FOR YOU.

EVERYTHING IMPORTANT IN THE EUROPEAN THEATER

OF OPERATIONS, WE HAVE BEEN THERE, MY BROTHER, RIGHT IN THE THICK OF IT. AND ON IT CONTINUES IN JUST THAT WAY UNTIL THE END. SO BE IT.

I LOVE MY PLANE AND I LOVE MY NOSE TURRET AND MY JOB. BILLY HARGREAVES GOT HIS RETRACTABLE BELLY TURRET, TOO, AND IT WAS GREAT FOR A WHILE. THEN ONCE, AFTER A MISSION, WE WERE WAITING OUT ON THE AIRFIELD LIKE WE DO WHEN IT'S EXTRA BAD. WAITING ON THE STRAGGLERS TO CHEER THEM ON HOME. AND THIS LIBERATOR, WOBBLING, LEAKING, SMOKING, IN BAD TROUBLE COMES INTO VIEW, AND WE CHEER THESE BOYS ON, AND WE SEE THEY GOT NO HYDRAULICS AT ALL, SO NO LANDING GEAR, NO RETRACTING THE RETRACTABLE TURRET UP FROM THAT BIG BELLY.

HAVE I TOLD YOU ABOUT THIS? HOW IT WORKS? GUY FOLDS AND SQUEEZES DOWN INTO POSITION IN THAT TUR-RET, WHICH CLOSES BEHIND HIM, AND THE WHOLE THING ROTATES SO HE CAN FACE THE FIGHTERS WITH HIS GUNS AND THERE IS NO MORE DOOR OPENING FOR HIM UP INTO THE PLANE WHILE HE IS IN SHOOTING POSITION. NOT UNTIL THE BALL ROTATES BACK UP, YOU SEE, AND THE DOOR PART MEETS UP WITH THE FUSELAGE OPENING.

ANYWAY, SO WE STOPPED CHEERING, OUT OF SHOCK, AND THEN WENT BACK TO CHEERING WHEN THE PLANE HAD NO CHOICE AND JUST CAME ON IN AND DOWN, THUMPING THEN SCRAPING WITH AN ALMIGHTY SCREECH INTO ONE SORRY MANGLING OF A BELLY LANDING.

SO BILLY HARGREAVES, ONCE NEARLY GETTING A NICKNAME OF BELLY BILLY, HE WAS LOVING THAT NEW TURRET SO MUCH, HE WAS ON THE GROUND CHEERING WITH US. THEN AFTER, HE DIDN'T LOVE IT SO MUCH. THEN, HE MADE A POINT OF TAKING A PISTOL WITH HIM ANY TIME HE HAD TO CLIMB BACK IN THERE BECAUSE HE SAID HE WASN'T EVER GOING TO SEE THE GROUND COME TO HIM LIKE THAT UNDER ANY CIRCUMSTANCES.

UNTIL FINALLY HE WOULDN'T GO DOWN IN THERE AT ALL. HE'S NOT FLAK-HAPPY OR LACKING MORAL FIBER OR LACKING ANYTHING ELSE. HE JUST COULDN'T GET HIMSELF DOWN INTO THAT BELLY BALL ONE MORE TIME, AS MUCH AS HE HAD LOVED IT ONCE. SO WE MADE ARRANGEMENTS, AND WOULD YOU CARE TO GUESS WHO HAS A NEW JOB, DOWN WHERE ALL THE ACTION REALLY IS?

SO, YOU WILL PROBABLY FALL EVEN FURTHER BEHIND, ADVENTURE-WISE, BUT WRITE. WRITE ANYWAY, BECAUSE NO

MATTER WHAT ANYBODY ELSE THINKS, YOU KNOW, AT LEAST
I WILL KEEP BEING INTERESTED.

AND, I BET YOU THOUGHT I WOULD FORGET. AM I
RIGHT?

HAPPY SECOND ANNIVERSARY, BROTHER. I HAVE TO
RUN NOW BECAUSE ADVENTURE CALLS AGAIN. I'LL WRITE
YOU ABOUT IT, AS LONG AS YOU KEEP WRITING, TOO.

JUNE 6, 1944

About the Author

Chris Lynch is the author of numerous acclaimed books for middle-grade and teen readers, including the Vietnam series and the National Book Award finalist *Inexcusable*. He teaches in the Lesley University creative writing MFA program and divides his time between Massachusetts and Scotland.